OUR FIELD TRIP - PG-13

BY CORNEL A. KEELER

www.trafford.com
North America & international
toll-free: 1 888 232 4444 (USA & Canada)
fax: 812 355 4082

This book is dedicated to several members of my family who have experienced the joys of teaching: My wife, Wanda; my daughters, Carmen and Tiffany; my sister, Marlene; and my cousins Delores and Wanda Jean.

For most students at East Orange Elementary School, this was just another school day.But not for the three fifth grade classes, for this was class trip day. I am one of theteachers, Mr. Wendell Carter.

East Orange County is a lot different from where I grew up. This is an upper middleclass area in southern California located away from the big cities and slightly removedfrom the rich and famous residents of Hollywood. Seventy percent of the students aredriven to school in cars.

I enjoy working here. The parents are so helpful and reliable. During open house thisyear, twenty-one of my twenty-five students were represented by at least one parent.

CHAPTER I

DURING THE SCHOOL YEAR we are required to take our classes on two educational trips, onecultural trip and one pleasure trip. Today is our pleasure trip.

This is my second year teaching at this school. With the money I'm making, I'llprobably retire at this job.

Originally, I was born and raised in Louisiana. If I had remained there and taught school, I would probably be earning fifty percent less than what I'm earning now.So my move to California was a financial advantage.

I grew up in Morgan City, Louisiana, a seafood and oil city. Morgan City is surroundedby water and is located only twenty miles from the Gulf of Mexico. Most of the majoroil companies opened facilities in Morgan City in the fifties and sixties. The oil industrycomplemented the seafood industry which had thrived there decades earlier. Just west ofMorgan City is a thriving sugar cane industry. At the height of what was known as the oilboom in the early seventies through the late eighties, Morgan City population was abouttwenty thousand. Jobs were readily available. I spent my summers working at Shell OilCompany or at the local hospital. The hospital job became my after school job duringmy senior year. The money I made was used for my future college expenses. The only regret I had was that I could not play football or basketball because of my night job. Thebest thing that came out of it was learning how to save and manage money and how to havecompassion for people.

The school I attended was a fun school. It was small and everyone knew everyone else.All of the students thought we had one of the best schools in the area academically.It took me only two weeks of college to realize how little I had been exposed to. The school was too small to incorporate all of the subjects taught at the larger schools, somany of the college preparatory courses weren't offered. Even though I graduated as anhonor student, my academic exposure was equivalent to that of a tenth grader at most ofthe larger schools. Most of our coaches were history of some other type or regularclassroom teacher with no training as a coach.

My parents were older than most of my classmate's parents. They weren't marrieduntil they were in their mid thirties. When I graduated form college, they were in theirsixties and had both retired. My sister Marion is two years older than me and my othersister Wilma is four years older. My parents decided that our first names would start with the same letters as theirs. My mother's name is Mildred and my dad's name isWardell. I don't know how my mother let dad get two W's as bossy as she is. My dad, whose nickname is Black, spent most of his life working on boats or doingjanitorial work. My mother worked in a seafood factory in her early years and finishedher work experience as a Head Start teacher. My parents were able to put both of my sisters through college. Of course they both helped themselves too with little jobs hereand there. My oldest sister Wilma is living in Monroe, La., and my other sister Marion isliving in Houston, Texas. Every year we meet at our parents' house for Thanksgiving.We usually spend the weekend after Thanksgiving in New Orleans at the Bayou Classic.In case you don't know what that is, it's a football game between Southern University andGrambling State University, with a host of other events surrounding the game. Eventhough I enjoy working in East Orange County, I miss Mardi Gras, music festivals andthe good Cajun food of my native state. Since moving to California, I have changed my eating habits. In visiting pizzerias here,I discovered that pineapple pizza was the favorite choice of the patrons as well asvegetable pizza. Back home pepperoni and meat lovers pizzas were the best sellers.

I also found that steak is popular in East Orange County, while seafood was a favoritedelicacy in Louisiana.

East Orange County restaurants sell shrimp, oysters and other seafood, but the prices areso high that people only buy them on special occasions.

In addition to eating habits, the people of East Orange County are different from mynative Louisianians in other ways.

I believe the differences in the two cultures are created by the differences in the typeof environment that each must live in. Even though different, each environment is goodif adapted to.

The people in East Orange County are real polite. They always tell me, "Good morningsir". You don't hear, "What's happening brother," like I would hear in Louisiana.

There is a night club located around the corner from my apartment. The clientelebuy mix drinks, mostly martinis and long island teas. Even the Blacks that patronize thebar, purchase similar drinks.

I usually purchase a couple of cold beers. I like my beer and those drinks are too damnexpensive.

Many of the people from Louisiana would be shocked to see how clean East Orange County is. People here just don't litter. They will fine your ass if they catch youlittering. They are serious about litter. There are little flowers all around the neutralgrounds, parks and public buildings. The trees are prettier than the ones back home. People in Louisiana like those big ugly, caterpillar filled oak trees, and want to lock youup if you cut one of them down.

In East Orange County, you can go to a park, lie under a palm tree, and view the snowcovered mountain peaks in the distance while bathing in the warm sun.

You are also just a short drive from some of the best beaches and some of the bestwine makers in the world.

Sometimes I get this superior feeling because I have lived in Louisiana and experiencedall the good things that the people enjoy in the great outdoors of the bayous, plus the great music and cuisine. These things most Californians know nothing about. By contrast,many Louisiana natives are not familiar with the beautiful flowers and plantsof California that are surrounded by rolling hills and snow capped mountains.

CHAPTER TWO

THIS MORNING WAS ROUTINE. I got up about 6:45, brewed some coffee and got ready forwork. I usually arrive at work around 7:45 A. M. This morning as soon as I pulled intothe parking lot, a duty teacher told me that the principal wanted to see me as soon aspossible.

I went to my classroom first and then to the office. Because of the trip, all of mystudents had to congregate in the gymnasium.

When I arrived at my classroom, Miss Turner and Mrs. Dorsey were already in thehallway discussing the seats we did not have.

"Good morning ladies."

Miss Turner, the older of the two, said, "Mr. Carter, don't you have a seven passengervan?"

"Yes I do," I replied.

Then she said, "If you use your van, that would solve our problem. The extra studentscould ride with you."

I paused for a moment. Then I asked, "What extra students?"

Mrs. Dorsey then explained that the two motor coaches could only transport 80passengers. We had 86 people scheduled to ride. She then said, "If you use your van,that would solve our problem. You could ride five of the students with you."

"Let me talk to Mrs. Williams first."

My van had new tires and had just been inspected.

Mrs. Williams was standing outside her office waiting for me. She had one of thoseconfused looks on her face.

"Good morning Mrs. Williams. I was told that you wanted to see me."

"Yes Mr. Carter," replied Mrs. Williams. "The bus drivers informed me that they couldnot carry as many people as we had listed. Mrs. Dorsey suggested that I ask you if youwould use your van to ride a few students."

My first thought was to say, "Hell no!" Riding on a bus or a motor coach, asMrs. Dorsey would say, leaving the driving to someone else was something I was lookingforward to. Driving was not something I wanted to do.

Mrs. Williams informed me that at least five students would have to ride with me. Shewent on further to say that four of the last students to commit were in my class, all girls.The fifth student was a boy from Miss Turner's class. She suggested that I take anothergirl instead of having one boy riding with a car full of girls.

After pausing for a while, I told her I would use my van. If I was going to have fivelittle girls in my van, it may as well be five who knew each other. I checked my list tosee which girl I would select from my class to ride with me. Of all the girls in my class,Diana was the next in line.

It was 8:00 A. M. After calling the roll, I had to check with each student to make surethey had at least thirty dollars with them. The thirty dollars was needed for them to eatwhile on the trip and maybe buy some souvenirs. After a short wait, Mrs. Williamswalked in and addressed the group. She basically talked about safety and aboutfollowing instructions. She presented me with a list of which students would be riding onthe first bus and which ones would be riding on the second bus. Mrs. Williams remindedthe students that the buses would be returning at 10:00 P. M.

After she finished talking, I called her to the side and asked if I could have a word withher. I thought about insurance. My van had full coverage insurance, but I wasn't sure ifthat included using it for a school trip.

"What can I help you with Mr. Carter?"

"Mrs. Williams, what about insurance?"

"The school's insurance will cover you on this trip. But, unfortunately in order to becovered, you have to drive a vehicle for hire. What that means is that the school willhave to compensate you for the use of your van."

"What about the parents? Are they comfortable with this?"

9

"Sure. You have a pretty good reputation at this school."

"Is there anything else Mr. Carter?" asked Mrs. Williams.

"If I think of something else, I'll call you before we leave."

Mrs. Williams headed to the parking lot where the buses were parked.

I walked back to the section of the gym where my class was seated. My classaddressed me again as they had a few moments earlier, "Good morning Mr. Carter."

"Good morning boys and girls."

They were all seated. I gave them their instructions for the trip. I then told them thatfive students would be riding with me in my van. Suddenly hands filled the air. Icouldn't believe they wanted to ride in and old Caravan instead of riding on a big bus.

I reminded them that the buses were first class motor coaches with radios, recliningseats and bathrooms. Most of the hands went down.

I then told them that the last five to have paid would ride with me. I checked the list toconfirm what Mrs. Williams had told me earlier that four girls in my class were the last topay their money for the trip. My list revealed that Cheryl, Kim, Patricia, Myrisha and Diana were the last five to pay. I informed the class that the five girls named would beriding with me.

As our departure time approached, the class lined up and proceeded to the boarding area.Mrs. Dorsey's and Miss Turner's classes were already at the buses when we arrived. Fiveminutes later, the buses were loaded with students, teachers and chaperones. The fivegirls and I had a few yards to walk to the other side of the parking lot where my van wasparked.

We loaded the van and pulled up behind the buses as they departed the school.

CHAPTER THREE

I WAS EXTREMELY EXCITED about this trip. All twenty-five of my students were going onthe trip. Three students in the other two classes were not going. They were Jehovah'sWitnesses and their parents wouldn't let them go.

My students are good kids. I believe the environment has something to do with theirbehavior. When I was in college, several of my professors stressed how importantdiscipline was in the classroom. I can remember Miss Dixon saying, "Before you canteach, you must have discipline."

The children all come from disciplined homes and this is reflected in theirconduct in the classroom. Most of these students are very polite and mannerable.Even the three Black girls in my class were not like the ones I was use to back inLouisiana. Whenever I mention my students to my girlfriend, she refers to themas the Cosby kids. I never have to yell at them. Sometimes I think this is whatit must be like at an acting school or on a Hollywood lot. Everyone seems to beplaying a role or seems to be in character.

Ten of my students are boys. Several boys in the other two fifth grade classeshave been trying to transfer to my class because they wanted a male teacher. Ourprincipal, Mrs. Ruth Williams wanted to place at least sixteen boys in my class.She said that a male authority figure would be good for them. However, the schoolboard said that all classes had to be divided evenly across gender lines. BeforeMrs. Williams became principal at East Orange, she was an assistant principalsomewhere in central Los Angeles. She probably had to deal with a different typeof product.

These students are constantly exposed to art and culture. They are probably morefamiliar with Pavarotti than with Elton John or Mark Anthony.

Even though these kids are all good students, I found them to be a little lessbroadminded and worldly than other children their age that I had been aroundpreviously.

Where I did my student teaching, the students were a little more sophisticated. In otherwords, some of them wore fad clothes, talked in slang, cursed, cut classes and didsome other things that may be considered more mainstream. These students in EastOrange County are angels.

At our school, we have two bells. The first bell sounds for the students to line up.Three minutes later the second bell sounds for the students to proceed to their classrooms.What's amazing about this school, each class has a designated area to line up. We onlyhave three duty teachers who handle the whole procedure. Each class proceeds to theirclassroom without being accompanied by their teacher. If this approach had been triedwhere I attended school, there would have been chaos and fights nearly every day.

East Orange Elementary has a waiting list of students wanting to attend and they don'thesitate to suspend or expel current students.

Back in Louisiana where I attended school, nearly everyone rode the bus to school orwalked. I guess it was more of a tradition than anything else. Or course I only livedfive blocks from school and there were several nice girls to walk to school with every day.

Now Josephine, she is just like the East Orange County people. She was raised inSan Jose in northern California. I don't think she tasted fried chicken until she was ateenager. Josephine is my lady friend. Her dad is a nurse at a hospital in San Jose and hermother is a real estate agent. I always kid her about her daddy being on the feminine side.

She always says, "He was man enough to make me."

Mr. and Mrs. Allen have been good to me since Josephine and I have been dating.Sometimes they remind me of my parents back in Louisiana. Once a month Josephineand I drive up to San Jose to visit her parents. We spend very little time at the house.We usually drive up to San Francisco to some restaurant or take a quick trip to Reno. Mr. Allen doesn't gamble. He just likes to eat.

Mrs. Allen is also from Louisiana like me. She is from New Orleans and calls herself a Creole queen. Mr. Allen is from the San Jose area. He complains all the time about hiswife's cooking. Mrs. Allen always cooks that spicy food. Sometimes she will cooka dish just for herself and me. Mr. Allen met Mrs. Allen in New Orleans when he wasthere for his internship.

Josephine and I met when she was in college. Her parents shipped her to hergrandmother's house in New Orleans after she finished high school and enrolled her intoDillard University. That is the same college her mother attended. I didn't attend Dillard.I graduated from Nicholls State University, a college about sixty miles from New Orleansin Thibodaux, Louisiana. One of my hometown guys got married and Josephine was oneof the maids. I was lucky enough to be her escort. I told her that we had a couple of thingsin common. We were both seniors and we were both Blue Devils. Both Dillard and myhigh school's mascot was the Blue Devil.

After the wedding we agreed to keep in touch. We eventually started dating. As weboth approached graduation, she would always invite me to move to California with her.I did.

She secured a job in East Orange County several months before she graduated fromcollege. When she got settled in her new job, she started looking for something for me.She phoned me and told me of several teacher openings in East Orange County. I wasthere within two days. She even secured an apartment for me across the street from hers.

This is our second year together. She said it would not look nice for us to live together.I never told her, but I wanted to have as much freedom as possible. Even though I lovedher very much, this was the first time in my life I had a car, money and an apartment. When she visited her parents alone, I would take advantage of my freedom.

Josephine majored in hotel management and is working as an assistant at an airporthotel. We are saving money to buy a house before we get married.

Last night I cooked her some jambalaya and fried some fish. She claimed she had todrink two Cokes because it was too spicy. She complains because I only buy Pepsi. Shetells me all the time that she does not like Pepsi. Once when she was visiting, I pouredthe Coke out of the bottle and refilled it with Pepsi. She never noticed the difference.Josephine is very product oriented. Maybe hotel management people are required to bechoosy about food since they serve the public.

Anyway, after dinner, I invited Josephine to spend the night. But she refused again as she always does. Even promising not to touch her did not work.

I knew I had a long day coming up tomorrow, so after that refusal, I rushed her out.After she left, I went to bed.

Josephine can be described as one of those good Catholic girls. She made me promiseto wait until after we were married to have sex. That did not bother me too much becausewe had a solid relationship and I was more in tune with her mind and personality.

In the past, some of my friends teased me because I wasn't horny all the time like theywere. Before Josephine, I dated several girls as friends. One of them was always idealfor dancing, partying, eating out, sporting events or just for sex.

I had a chance to meet a couple of guys that Josephine had dated previously, one incollege and one back in her home town.

They were okay guys, but I thought Josephine was too much woman for them. I justhope she is not too much woman for me.

CHAPTER FOUR

WE WERE HEADED for the mountains to visit an underground cavern, a tropical gardenand an amusement park. The three and a half hour drive would put us at the first stoparound noon.

We instructed the bus drivers to stop at a roadside park that was about three hoursinto the trip, to allow everyone an opportunity to stretch and use the restroom. The parkhad a small snack bar. Surprisingly, only a few of the children bought food from thesnack bar, especially since there were no picnic baskets or ice chests on the buses.

The girls didn't get out of the van. During the trip from the school, they slept most ofthe way. When they were awake, they mainly compared grandmothers and discussed, "TheYoung and the Restless."

The caverns didn't have any real food, only chip and candy vending machines. But thetropical gardens had a restaurant on site. This is where we were going to eat our lunch.We were scheduled to arrive there about 2:00 P. M.

It was a beautiful day to travel. The temperature was about 75 degrees and there wasn't a cloud in the sky.

After we left the roadside park, it took only twenty minutes to reach the cavern site.The students were getting real excited at this point. So was I. This would be my secondtime visiting a cavern. After visiting relatives in Baltimore with my parents, we stoppedand toured a cavern in Tennessee, and one around Shenandoah, Virginia, during our tripback home. The trip was my high school graduation gift.

Mrs. Dorsey gave instructions to all the students on how to act and how they would proceed through the cavern. The five girls riding in my van quickly vanished into thecrowd of students.

The students lined up in rows of two at the entrance and waited for the tour guides.When the tour guides arrived, they divided us up into three groups of about twenty-nineeach.

Miss Turner and I toured with the first group.

The cavern called the LaCasa cavern, consisted of a single chamber, and was onlymoderately deep.

The cave revealed and assortment of underground landscapes filled with beautifulodd shaped mineral deposits.

LaCasa has a lake and several waterfalls. The cavern featured what looked like artformed from limestone, marble and dolomite. Icicle like formations hung from theceiling with flower like gypsum stones in the foreground of what looked like draperiesmade of flowstone. The colors, mostly light green, gold and ice blue marble, made anenormous impression.

The tour through the cavern took about an hour. Most of the children had never seenan underground cavern before and were fascinated. The temperature was about 50degrees in the cavern and most of us were a little cold, especially since most of us werewearing shorts.

As we completed the tour, we were put on an elevator, fifteen at a time and taken up tothe ground level. A souvenir shop awaited us as we arrived at the exit. Nearly everyonewanted at least one souvenir to take back home. It took about 35 minutes for everyoneto make their purchases and return to the buses.

We departed the cavern at 1:30. We were scheduled to be at the tropical gardens for2:00 P. M.

As we traveled between stops, the girls were both chastising and envying Myrisha forbuying so many souvenirs. She purchased thirteen souvenirs that cost well over ahundred dollars.

Myrisha's father is an attorney for a large law in the Los Angeles area. His clientlist includes several actors, athletes and some corporate types. In other words, he bringshome a lot of bacon. Myrisha's mother operates a dress shop in the plush OrangeBlossom Mall. She sells Sax Fifth Avenue and Macy's type clothes. She even uses hershop for direct sales of designer originals.

Josephine took me to that shop once. I remember looking at a dress selling for $16,000.Myrisha of course, is the best-dressed girl in my class. She has a habit of daydreaming. Ialways thought, maybe she's thinking about what to buy next. Occasionally, she would bedropped off at school in her father's limo. He uses it a lot in his business. In spite of herwealth, she is a sweet kid, not spoiled or snobbish at all. Academically, she is just abovean average student.

Myrisha spends a lot of time with her nanny. This lady picks her up from school mostdays, because her parents are so busy. She says that her nanny takes care of her andteaches her all about life. Myrisha's family wanted to supply all of the food for ourChristmas party, but I wouldn't allow that.

The school receives a substantial donation from Myrisha's parents every year to be used at the discretion of the principal.

Myrisha apparently spends a lot of money on clothes. When your mother owns a dress shop, clothes are pretty easy to come by.

Patricia's clothes, on the other hand, are not up to par with the other girls. Her mothermakes most of her clothes and they really look homemade. Based on the way herclothes fits, her mother must make them exact. They are always tight fitting and showher curves.

As we approached the Pacific Gardens, it became evident that I would have to stop andbuy some gas. I only had a quarter of a tank remaining. If I had known I was going to beusing my van, I would have filled up last night. We had just passed two gas stations, butthey were the discount kind. The last time I used some of that discount gas, my vanstarted bucking, and that was on a flat surface. I knew I couldn't use it in the mountains.Whatever type of gas I buy, the school is going to pay for the gas anyway.

We finally reached the gardens. I had been here several times before and didn't reallywant to go in, so I didn't. My passengers went in with one of the parents and the othertwo teachers.

The two bus drivers and I went across the street from the gardens to a coffee shop.They bought coffee and ham sandwiches while

I bought a cheeseburger with fries and aPepsi. I really had a desire for some donuts and milk, but I knew I could not drink milkwith those five girls riding with me in my van. If I'd cut one loose, they would have a field day with me back at school.

The two bus drivers finished before I did and returned to their buses. I stayed awhile and chatted with the waitress. She was one of those fat funny women. She had allkinds of stories about her and her man.

I slipped in a few words about my squeeze too. But she wasn't interested in Josephine.She wanted to know more about me. Her name was Mable. She wanted to know howlong I had been teaching and if I was a good teacher.

I told her that I was in my second year teaching. "So far it's been a great job. Myprincipal, Mrs. Williams, gave me an excellent evaluation. I kid with her often about hername, because my high school principal had the exact same name, Ruth Williams." I toldher that I had become one of the most popular teachers at the school. "I guess being theonly male teaching at the fifth grade level and lower has a lot to do with it."

After glancing through a newspaper, I went back to my van. By this time the otherswere eating in the restaurant. I turned the switch on, slipped in a CD and started listingto some music.

The others started coming out of the restaurant one by one. Cheryl was the first of myriders to appear. She went and sat on a bench and waited for the others.

Cheryl and her parents previously lived in Los Angeles, but moved to East OrangeCounty where there is a little more space. Cheryl qualified to run for class presidentbut withdrew because of her schedule. Cheryl plays in the school band, plays on the basketball team, and is one of the fancy dancers on our school's dance team. Inaddition, she is an honor student.

Cheryl is very mannerly. She never fails to say, "Good morning Mr. Carter." Sheis also one of my best chess players. She tells me that she wants to be a first gradeteacher when she finishes college. One day I asked her, "Don't you think you're a littleyoung to be thinking about a career and college?"

She said, "No."

What really fascinates me about her college ambition is that she wants to go to atraditionally Black college in the South. She has mentioned Tuskegee and Florida A. & M.I learned that her father was from Mississippi and once played saxophone in theJackson State University marching band. I am sure that much of her interest in the Southcomes from her father's experiences and stories.

Her dad works as a car sales consultant and plays music on weekends at different clubsin the area. Her mother is an assistant manager at a local dollar store. I was surprisedto discover that there was a dollar store in East Orange County. We only have oneWal-Mart and it's not even a super center.

Cheryl is one of only five Black students in my class. I know teachers aren't supposeto have favorites, but if I had a daughter, I would like for her to be just like Cheryl. Sheis tall and has a wonderful smile. Cheryl is not a bad looking little girl. I wonder how shewould look with a different hairstyle. She's worn the same one everyday this school year.,

As the last of the group exited the restaurant, I was called to take a picture. Several ofmy students wanted to take pictures with me. There were several backdrops withpictures of flowers, fruits and birds. I posed for several pictures with groups and withindividuals. However, none of the five girls riding with me were included in any of thepicture taking. "Uh," I thought to myself. "I guess they don't like the way I drive"

Mrs. Dorsey and Miss Turner also came over to where I was seated and asked me to takea picture with them. They wanted to use the entrance to the gardens as a back drop.

The entrance was surrounded by a series of roses and rhododendron bushes, and withsmall gardens filled with a mixture of hibiscus, golden poppy, peony and iris plants.

When the girls got back into the van, Patricia had a small salad with her and a diet soda.When she noticed me staring, she said she didn't eat in the restaurant and decided to waituntil we got back on the road.

"Is that all you're going to eat?" I asked.

She said she had to watch her weight. She said her mother tells her she is getting fat.

Actually she is getting fine. Even though she is only twelve, she has the body of afifteen or sixteen year old. She is well developed.

Compared to the other girls, Patricia is a little naïve. She grew up very poor along witha little brother and sister. Her brother's name is Lesley and her sister's name is Jessie.That causes confusion sometimes. Her father was a heavy drinker and was killed in an auto accident when she was seven years old. He was found one morning with his truckwrapped around a tree.

Her mother remarried. She was working at a supermarket as a cashier when she mether current husband. He was an insurance man who shopped at the supermarketregularly, but who was also a widower. He is twelve years older than Patricia's mother.He lost his first wife to cancer. They have been married to each other for three years.Patricia is very appreciative of her new life. Her stepfather buys her anything she wants.He takes her and the family to church every Sunday and to parks, movies, museums andother attractions every weekend. Patricia tells me how happy she is. They moved from athree-room house to a seven-room house with four bedrooms. Patricia loves to talk abouthow she decorates her room. She is one happy little girl.

Sometimes I've had to talk to some of the boys about looking at her in a certain way orsaying things to her that they shouldn't say. Personally I would say to myself, "I surewould like to see her when she's twenty-one."

CHAPTER FIVE

OUR LAST STOP was the amusement park. The park was a small park consisting mostly ofroller coasters. We arrived at the park around 4:30 P. M.

The park wasn't too busy. We were able to go through the rides rather fast. We werescheduled to remain at the park until 6:00 P. M. Most of the people in this area visitDisneyland and Knott's Berry Farm. Then most patrons don't come to amusement parksuntil school is out.

I didn't ride while at the park. I was tempted to ride in the bumper cars, but there wereno other adults riding. The children were riding the roller coasters and having a great time.

As I was walking through the park, I spotted Diana setting on a bench reading a book.I approached her and said, "Diana, you're suppose to be having fun, not readinga book."

Diana replied, "Mr. Carter, you might not understand, but reading is my favorite thingto do."

"Well you continue reading," I replied.

"I'm going to Disneyland next month with my mother and I'll get lots of chances toride."

I said, "Good," and then walked away.

Diana has never made lower than an A in her first five years of school. Back inOctober of last year, Diana informed me that she had read all her textbooks from cover tocover, and we were only three weeks into the school year. Whenever I assign work to theclass, she is usually the first one to finish. To keep Diana and the other early finishersoccupied, I allow them to play challenging games such as chess and do crosswordpuzzles, etc.

She is the only student to checkmate me. She loves chess and thanks me frequently forteaching the game to her. Miss Turner told me one time that she saw Diana at the beautyshop reading a book. I guess she takes one with her everywhere she goes.

Diana belongs to a tutoring club. They spend time after school two days a week helpingstudents in lower grades with their studies and with their homework. Diana is also the quietest student in the class. She says very little.

Diana comes from a single parent home. Her mother doesn't look much older thanDiana. Her mother is in her late twenties and works as a waitress in a gentlemen's club.I have never heard her mention her father.

Diana, according to a class project earlier this year, says she wants to be a doctor.

At 6:00 P. M. everyone headed for the buses. The five girls and I walked to the van.The buses had separate loading and unloading areas from other vehicles.

When we boarded the van, Kim got into the front seat this time. Previously all the girlsrode in the second and third seats. She said, "I'm going to ride up here with you to makesure you don't go to sleep."

I have never seen Kim's father, but she didn't look like her mother. Her mother was abrunet and Kim had black hair with blue eyes. She is the prettiest girl in the class andmaybe in the entire school. Nearly all the little boys are in love with her.

However, she hasn't developed an interest in boys yet. She is still concerned about herclass work and girl friends. Kim is one of my better students.

Despite being very friendly, some of the girls tease her because of the way she looks.They say, "You think you're cute" or, "You think you're too good for us."

Despite their feelings, it appears the other girls enjoy being in her company. At recess,she is always surrounded by a group of girls.

Kimberly complains sometimes about other girls playing in her hair. She has a full headof long black hair. She is a little hairy too.

This is Kimberly's first year at East Orange Elementary School. She transferred in fromsome small town in Colorado. Her father works for an oil company and moves aroundfrom time to time. Her mother is just a homemaker who spends hours each day in theyard working her flower gardens. She has won the garden of the month twice by twodifferent organizations.

It was time to head back home. We took a different route going home. The tripactually took us in an oval or a near circle. Our school was four hours from theamusement park going in the direction we were heading.

Before we left, I told the bus drivers that I had to stop for gas. They volunteered to stopand wait for me, but I told them not to, because I didn't want them to arrive at the schoolany later than 10:00 P. M.

"I'll catch up later."

About twenty minutes from the park, I saw a Chevron sign. So I headed to the station.The Chevron station was three blocks off of the main highway. After gassing up wedrove off. At this time we were about fifteen minutes behind the buses.

The girls wanted me to speed so that we could catch and pass the buses and beat themback to school.

The girls started singing songs, so I turned he radio off. About fifteen minutes fromthe service station, I felt a vibration coming from the van. Up ahead I saw some rocksfalling.

Cheryl yelled, "I think it's an earthquake!"

I quickly pulled the van off the highway on to a clearing away from the right side of theroad where the rocks were coming from. I pulled up behind some trees. The girls were screaming and hugging each other. Kim was helping me with directions. We were tryingto find the safest place to park away from the falling rocks.

Suddenly we could see rocks falling from the top of the mountainside ahead of us. I was getting real concerned. There was a narrow stretch of road about 50 yards ahead of usthat was bordered by the mountain on both sides. As the rocks continued to fall, they-began to fill up the opening. I knew we were going to have to turn around and goback the other way.

After about two minutes, the rumbling from the avalanche was over. Immediately Irealized that the road ahead was blocked. I turned the radio back on. The station wasindeed reporting an earthquake in the Burbank area. According to the radio station, theearthquake was a 5.3 on the Richter scale. I told the girls to remain in the van and keepthe doors locked. I left the window cracked on the driver's side with my keys in theignition.

As I exited the van, I could still feel it rocking, but this time it was from the brisk wind.

I walked about twenty yards ahead of the van toward the area where the rocks had beenfalling. The fallen rocks and boulders had blocked the passageway. They were piled upsomewhere around sixty feet high. The mountain wall stood at least a half mile up onthe right where the rocks had come from to about ninety feet on the left.

I turned around and walked back toward the van.

To the south were several more trees. I decided to take a look in that direction.The clearing ended only thirty yards from where the van was parked. When I got to theedge, I looked down and saw a valley that dropped for hundreds and hundreds of feet, avalley of wild brush and trees.

I then turned my attention back toward the direction of the service station, or from thedirection we had just come from. I had walked back about a quarter of a mile before Iheard what sounded like running water. A few more steps and I could see what lookedlike a small creek flowing across the highway where we had just passed. The road hadbeen washed away. The stream appeared to be sixty to seventy feet wide and was rushing down toward the valley to the south.

We were trapped.

I made my way back to the van where the girls were still locked in. As I approachedthe van I started thinking about God and Jesus. After seeing those falling boulders andthe rushing water behind me, but for the grace of God those rocks could have come down on us, or we could have been swept away by the powerful waterfall that developedbehind us.

When I reached the van, Kimberly reached over and opened the door. I enlightened themto what I had experienced around the perimeter of the van. They didn't say a word. Theyjust stared at me, at each other and then into space.

"You know how lucky we are, don't you?"

The girls all gave some type of affirmative answer.

I asked them to individually thank God for sparing us and to protect us until we can getsafely home.

Each girl seemed to have been praying silently for about a minute. Then Cherylstarted praying out aloud. She prayed as though she had spent some time in church. Shewas thanking the Lord for everything and asking Him for multiple favors. I was proud ofwhat she was doing, even though it was a little irritating to me. She was saying, "OurFather," after every few words. She reminded me of an old Baptist deacon from backhome. By the time he would finish blessing the food, the ice would be melted in our icetea.

One of those "Our Fathers," however, got my attention. She expressed her confidencein Him that he had protected the students, teachers and parents on the two buses that weretraveling ahead of us.

She even included a little part specifically for me.

In the drama that had befallen us, I had not thought about the two buses. I haddirected all my thoughts and prayers to the five little girls who were in my care.

As we sat in the van, I knew the people on the buses and the people back at schoolwere worrying about us. Suddenly, I remembered seeing one of the girls talking on a cellphone earlier.

"Which one of you has a cell phone?"

"I have one," replied Myrisha. "Call your parents and let them know that we are okay!"

Suddenly Kimberly, in a voice of desperation, yelled for everyone to be quiet. Theradio station was reporting on our field trip group.

According to the radio report, the twobuses had made it safely out of the mountains and were headed to the school. Then thereport said that our van was missing with a teacher and five students. Mrs. Dorsey hadphoned the principal, Mrs. Williams and had given her all the details. The report said thatwe were in the vicinity of the ava-lanche and may have met with tragedy or we could betrapped.

The girls seemed to be very excited about being talked about on the radio. They startedsaying stupid things about how the President would send troops to rescue us, and whatthey were going to wear when they are interviewed on Oprah.

Myrisha said, "Oh it's going to be so hard to decide what to wear."

I again asked Myrisha to call her parents.

She said, "Okay, okay, okay!"

Myrisha didn't seem to be concerned all of a sudden. All five girls seem to have madea 180-degree turnaround since they heard the radio report concerning our whereabouts.

After several attempts, Myrisha informed us that she was not getting a signal.

The radio station report said a helicopter would be dispatched as soon as possible.High winds associated with a late season cool front had brought with it some very strong upper level winds.

Diana then suggested that we try to make the call from outside the van over by the edgeof the cliff. "Why not?"

Everyone exited the van and walked toward the edge of the cliff. Myrisha dialed hermother's number again. This time she got a ring. A frighten mother answered the phone.

"Myrisha, is that you?"

"Yes Mother."

"Are you okay? Where are you? Are you hurt?"

"Everyone is okay Mother. We are trapped between a rock fall and a washed outhighway."

"Where is Mr. Carter?"

"He's right here."

"Let me talk to him."

"My mom wants to talk to you."

"Mrs. Moore, this is Mr. Carter."

"Mr. Carter, tell me what is going on? What happened? Where are you?"

"Mrs. Moore, we are in the mountains about 170 miles from the school. There was a rockslide ahead of us that blocked the road. We pulled off the road away from the side of the mountain. We later discovered that the road behind us had washed away also. We will have to be rescued eventually. We are on Highway 117 about twenty miles from the Chevron service station on Vista Road. There is an opening near where the water is flowing to land a helicopter."

"Mr. Carter, you are cutting out. You said something about a highway?"

"Yes! We are on Highway 117 about twenty miles from Vista Road. Talk to the bus drivers."

"Highway 117?"

"Yes! Tell Mrs. Williams!"

Suddenly, all I could hear was some noise coming from the other end of the phone. Myrisha said that the batteries were getting weak. She said the red indicator light had come on.

We weren't sure how much info Mrs. Moore had understood other than we were okay.

I returned her cell phone and suggested that we head back to the van. It had gotten dark. I became worried because we were isolated and I didn't know what was out there. Myrisha was the first student to arrive at the van. She opened the front passenger door and sat in the front seat where Kimberly had been sitting previously.

I reached under my seat and pulled out a little case. I always carried a gun in my van. The school board recommended that each school have a security team. Each team member had a permit to carry a gun. We were allowed to bring it to school, but it had to be locked up at all times. My gun case had two locks on it. I hope I don't ever have to use it. It'll take me too long to get to it and be in a position to use it.

I turned the radio on again. The station was playing classical music. The announcersaid, "Stay tuned for the news at the top of the hour." The girls were all resting or tryingto take a nap. I turned the volume down low hoping it would not disturb them.

Suddenly there was an aftershock. Rocks could be seen falling ahead kicking up dust,as some of them exploded into smaller pieces. The noise was greater than the first time.The roar sounded like the wind during the height of a hurricane back home. Imagine atrain or jet plane stationary over the roof of our house.

Concern grew as the rocks began to come closer to our parking spot. One tire size rockmanaged to slip between the two trees that were protecting us and hit the side of the van.

Myrisha, apparently frightened by the event crossed over and attached her arms aroundmy neck as she took a seat on my lap. I immediately hugged her and tried to reassure herthat everything would be okay. It didn't seem important at the time, but I knew that rockhad put a dent in the side of my van.

Moments after the vibrating and rumbling stopped, Myrisha slowly released me andmoved back into the passenger seat.

The aftershock seemed to have frightened as well as energized the girls. Cherylsuggested that I change the radio station to a station with some livelier music.

"Let's listen to the news first, then you can change the station."

The music on the radio was competing with the blistering sound of water, which seemed tohave develop some type of rhythm as it poured across the road. Staring in the directionof the water, it appeared to be getting closer. It was a good time to check out the water.As I exited he van, I could see the water glowing under the moonlight. The make shiftwaterfall had alarmingly come closer.. The area had expanded some twenty-five to thirtyyards. Our football field size opening had suddenly become an opening of only aboutseventy-five yards.

Scenes like this have been common in California during the spring rainy season, whenyou can see houses falling down from the hilltops.

Not being from California I did not know much about mud slides. Nonetheless, my comfort zone was suddenly being dismantled. It was scary not knowing how close thewater would come to the van.

I headed back to the van. I got in the van, started the engine and moved the van upcloser to the rocks located in front of the van.

Kim asked, "Why are you moving the van?"

"The water is coming closer from the rear. I'm just trying to be safe."

In my mind, I was thinking that we might be here longer than I had first thought.

Then the radio station was on and was mentioning our trip and that we were involvedin the earthquake. They reported that the buses and everyone on them were safe. Theysaid that the buses would arrive at the school around 10:30 P. M. The station thenreported that a van driven by a Mr. Carter had stopped for gas and was not with thebuses. They reported that the van contained five students and had not been heard fromand was missing. The report said the sheriff would be dispatching a rescue party atdaylight to search for the missing van. They reported that high winds and roadconditions created by the earthquake made it unsafe at the current time.

The girls gave what I sensed to be a humorous cheer. They seem to enjoy beingin the spotlight.

Suddenly, I realized that I didn't tell Mrs. Moore to call Josephine.

I then asked Myrisha to use her phone. Instead of passing me her cell phone, sheasked, "Who are you going to call?"

I said, "Miss Allen. I'll ask her to call the radio station to let them know that we are allokay, and to let her know that I'm okay."

Kimberly, with a big smile and her baby blue eyes staring at me, said, "Girls he'stalking about Josephine."

Myrisha paused. "Josephine?" I'm not going to use up my battery so you can call yourlittle girlfriend."

Kimberly added, "You don't need to call Josephine. Let her listen to the radio."

I wouldn't admit it out aloud, but Myrisha was correct. We could probably get only onemore call out of the cell phone, and we may need that for the rescue party in the morning.Myrisha didn't bring her plug in chord with her, so we couldn't charge the phone. Then Cheryl said, "We don't need to call the radio stations. They can't do anythingfor us anyway."

Then from the back seat, Patricia, seemingly representing the consensus feeling of theothers remarked, "I don't mind being missing as long as I'm not really missing."

As I sat and listened, the girls got into a round robin discussion about how theirclassmates, schoolmates and the people in the community must be thinking about them.They were talking about how many people and T. V. cameras were going to be at the school to greet them.

After listing to this for about twenty minutes, I turned the radio up.It is times like this that I question my kindness by agreeing to use my van. My bestfriend back in college would have told Mrs. Williams, "Hell no! Only my honeys ride inmy chariot." Of course Johnel would not be driving a mini-van. He would probably bedriving a Corvette or Mustang.

Thinking to myself, "Maybe I ought to ditch this van and buy a small sports car.Then only Josephine and I could ride. But I need something that I can haul things in. Asmall pick-up truck would probably be better."

My thought pattern was broken when one of my all time favorite songs came on theradio. It was an old Joe Tex song. "Someone to Take Your Place." I started singingsome of the lyrics from the song real softly.

"I didn't write you to, talk about the weather, I'm writing to say that I found someone,to take your place. Now how you like that baby."

"Excuse me Bobby Brown," uttered Diana from the back seat.

I'm thinking to myself, "No she didn't!"

Before I could answer, Cheryl, laughing loudly, said, "Girl that is Joe Tex."

"Who?" Diana yells loudly, trying to communicate with Cheryl over the volume on theradio plus my self-pleasing vocalization.

Diana spends so much time reading, she probably doesn't know anything about music.She probably would make a B in one of her courses if she would listen to too muchmusic.

Rich families like Myrisha's probably only listen to classical music. Myrisha, beingan average student, would have a hard time grasping the complexity of classical music,but that is probably the only type of music they have in the mansion.

"Mr. Carter, all these California girls know is the Beach Boys."

"Cheryl, how do you know about Joe Tex?"

"My dad has a collection of old records that he plays all the time. The band he playswith practices at the house sometimes and my mom and I pretend we are nightclubsingers." Cheryl continued, "My mom likes to play Tina Turner so she can shake infront of my dad. He doesn't like her to do it in front of the band members. Hedoesn't want me to shake at all, but I do when he's not around."

"Hey!" yelled Diana. "I hate to interrupt your little conversation, but I have to go to thebathroom."

"Diana," as I turned down the volume on the radio, "You're going to have to go behindone of those trees."

Diana started moving toward the door asking each of the other girls if they wanted toaccompany her. She said she did not want to go alone.

None of the girls budged. So I asked Kimberly to go with her.

She hesitated, rolled her eyes at me, and then slowly got out of the van and went withDiana.

"Why don't you put your headlights on them so they can see where they are going,"uttered Myrisha.

"Yes, why don't you Mr. Carter?" Addressing Myrisha and Patricia, "Girls, there is enough moonlight out there for themto see all they need to see."

31

"Why didn't you go with her Mr. Carter?"

This time Myrisha asked what I thought was a dumb question. She was still in thefront passenger seat that had been previously occupied by Kimberly.

I did not respond to Myrisha's question. I just started getting into the music. I startedsnapping my fingers and bobbing my head to the beat of the song on the radio.Myrisha, addressing her comments to the other two girls seated behind her, "If that wasJosephine, he would have gone."

I continued to ignore Myrisha's comments.

It had been a few minutes since Diana and Kimberly left and now they were returning.

I was tired sitting down and my legs were beginning to cramp up. There was nothingto do. As they got back to the van, I decided I would take a walk. By this time the temperaturehad dropped. It must have been somewhere in the sixties. Everyone had on long sleeved tops or had bought along a windbreaker. Everyone had been asked to wearlong sleeves or bring a sweater or windbreaker with them because of the temperatureon the buses.

I walked over to the edge of the cliff. I heard someone coming behind me.

"Mr. Carter, may I ask you something?"

"Sure," I replied.

"Why did you ask me to go with Diana instead of one of the other girls?"

Kimberly had departed the van and followed me to the edge of the cliff. At that momentI believed that I should receive some additional compensation when I return to school.Spending a night in the mountains with a bunch of silly little girls is not in my jobdescription.

After a brief pause, I turned to Kimberly and simply stated that she was asked becauseshe was the kindest of the group.

Kimberly, no longer standing by my side, but now facing me with her back to the edge ofthe cliff, stood staring me straight in the eyes.

"I thought you were trying to get rid of me. After all, you let Myrisha sit in my frontseat."

"Your front seat?"

"Kimberly, it doesn't matter to me which one of you occupies the front seat. I just wanteveryone to be safe and as comfortable as possible."

The word safe suddenly reminded me that I had left my gun in the van with the caseunlocked.

After a brief, tense moment, I relaxed. I remembered putting it in the glovecompartment with my checkbook and locking it up.Kimberly had said something else to me, but I wasn't listening. She must have sensedthat my mind had drifted for a moment.

Suddenly, she grabbed one of my hands. Then in an unusually soft voice, she asked,"Wendell, are you okay?"

I quickly pulled my hand from her grasp, and turned toward the van to see if any of theother girls had seen that. It was too dark, even though the moon was providing muchneeded light as it cast a shadow over the landscape. I was becoming less and lesscomfortable with the girls leaving the protection of the van. Another big after-shockcould trigger another rock slide that could put them in danger. Plus the waterfallbehind us was slowly creeping closer and closer. I had faith in God that we wouldbe protected, but I was wondering if the van was in the safest spot. I didn't want thegirls to know how worried I was, but I had decided to keep them close to the van.

This was my first earthquake and I wasn't as comfortable with my decisions as I wouldbe during a hurricane.

Before I could gather my thoughts to say anything, Kim said, "I bet you wish you werehere with Josephine instead of me."

"I wish I was back at home with Josephine."

"Do you think Josephine is as pretty as me?"I'm thinking now that I need to shut off this conversation as quickly as possible.

"Kimberly, Josephine is a beautiful woman. When you get older, you'll probably lookalmost as good as she does, that's if you take care of yourself."

"Bull shit!" she yelled.

I then turned back around and looked at Kimberly. She had a big smile on her face. Thestrands of her hair had been separated by the brisk wind and were hanging wildly on hershoulders. Indeed she was one of the prettiest females I had ever seen. If she was ten years older,even if I was married, I believe I would have grabbed her and held her in my arms.

With that thought, I believed it was time to go back to the van, hoping that being in thepresence of the other girls would change her mood.

I turned and started walking toward the van and she quickly followed. Half way to thevan, she slapped me on my butt.

While still walking, I turned and looked at her. My emotions were high. I knew that thiswas a problem I had to deal with. Two options came to mind. One was to slap her, andmaybe she would stop acting in this manner and act like the girl I had grown to know. And the other was threaten to tell her parents.

But I knew the first option wouldn't go over too well.

Before we reached the van, she got in another jab at Josephine.

"If I was older Wendell, I know I could take you from Josephine. I can tell by the wayyou look at me that you love me."

Not sure what to say, I opened the door to the van and attempted to get in. Suddenly,Kimberly pushed me backwards and jumped into the driver's seat. I closed the door behindher and walked around to the passenger side and got in. Myrisha had moved from the front seat back to the second row seat that she had occupied for most of the trip.

The atmosphere in the van was strained. No one said anything. The radio was on with acountry and western song vibrating from the speakers.

After about five minutes, Patricia opened the door.

"Where are you going?" I asked as the silence was broken.

"I'm going pee."

Myrisha and Cheryl also left the van. As all three girls headed for one of the trees nearthe edge of the cliff, I was glad Diana was still in

34

the van. She was, however, on the backseat.

Kimberly then reached over and placed her hand on my leg.

I quickly removed her hand. Out of the corner of my eyes, I could see her staringat me. Those big blue eyes seem to be glowing.

I asked her to get out of the drivers seat.

"Why," she asked.

"I want to start the engine to make sure the radio isn't running the battery down."

She hesitated, and then opened the door.

"Don't call me Kimberly, call me Kim."

The overhead light illuminated the front passenger seat. Kim was staring in the area of my waistline.

I glanced downward and noticed that my penis was pushing against my pants leg asthough it was searching for a way out. I took my hands, covered it over and pushed itdown so that it wouldn't be noticed at a glance.

Kim's eyes traveled from my pelvic area to my face. She smiled as though she hadaccomplished something. She closed the door and ran toward the area where the threeother girls were.

I was wondering about her state of mind. Did she feel angry or rejected? What will shetell the other girls? I didn't want to get accused of doing anything wrong.

Even though I'm not a Catholic Priest, the type of bad publicity that surrounded themcould also haunt me if Kim accuses me of something.

The van started up okay. I turned the radio off and put on a tape. It was a bluestape consisting of various artist including Bobby Bland and Clarence Carter.

Diana moved from the back seat to the second seat. She didn't say anything.

I saw the other four girls headed toward the running water behind the van.

I yelled and told them to be careful. Even though I felt safe in this area, I decided toopen the glove compartment and check my gun.

Diana, breaking the silence, said, "Why do you have that gun?"

Sarcastically I replied, "I need it to protect me from robbers."

"Isn't it true that most people who own guns end up killing some-one they know?"

"No," I replied. "Many people who get killed are usually killed by someone theyknow. Most people who own guns don't kill anyone."

I'm not the type to defend owning a gun. I hate guns. But the school board came upwith a plan to help protect the students and the school in the event of some attemptedtakeover, or an incident like the one in Colorado.

Because there weren't too many males working on campus, I felt slightly obligated toparticipate in the program.

They provided me with firearms training and gave me the op-tion to keep it in my car orin the classroom. They built a special safe in the walls of a few classrooms for the guns.I was sworn in as a licensed deputy sheriff with my jurisdiction limited to the campus. The school board did not provide us with guns, but they do pay us a small monthly fee.

If I had been in some of those Los Angeles school districts, I would not have done it. But in East Orange, I didn't expect any trouble. East Orange County only had onemurder last year. Some woman shot and killed her husband because she caught another-woman driving her Jaguar. But you never can tell, some little rich white boys mightdecide to go off one day on their schoolmates, some of Myrisha's little rich friends.

I continued to listen to the blues. I had recorded various artists on the same cassette.

"Mr. Carter, when I finish college, I'm going to run for congress. I'm going to makethings better for people, especially women."

With that statement, Diana really threw me. I just knew she was going to sayminorities. Then maybe she wasn't aware that Blacks and Hispanics living only a fewmiles from her, were living in poverty and crime stricken neighborhoods whereunemployment was over fifteen percent.

"What about helping some of the other minorities?"

Diana replied, "You're talking about welfare, aren't you?"

"No! There are problems that have nothing to do with welfare. Anyway welfare is apolitical thing. Politicians use the welfare program to provide jobs to both their familymembers and friends and the family members and friends of their supporters. Overseventy percent of the money spent goes to the operation of this program. What is notwell known is that most of the people on welfare are white people."

Diana laughed. "Mr. Carter so you expect me to believe that? Every time I see a storyabout welfare on T. V., it's always Blacks and Mexicans that are being interviewed."

I thought this would be a good opportunity to educate at least one student. "Miss Stevens, before 1964, America separated Blacks and whites, especially in theSouth. Whites had good schools with new textbooks, while Blacks had bad schools withold textbooks from white schools after they had been used for three to ten years. Awhite school would receive $10,000 from their school board for it's basketball team and aBlack school would receive only $2,500 to nothing at all. White schools offered coursesin accounting, physics, chemistry I and II, trigonometry, psychology, French, Spanish aswell as other courses that were not taught in the black schools. Some white schoolseven taught political science. The teachers were even paid more at a white school thanteachers at Black schools."

"Blacks were not taught the importance of voting, how to vote, whom to vote for, orwhy to vote."

"When Blacks were given the right to vote, the Democratic Party was in office, so theyregistered and voted Democratic automatically. I know a guy back home who says hewouldn't vote for his mother if she was a Republican."

Diana interrupted, "Are you a Democrat?"

"Yes I am, but I vote Republican sometimes. I vote for ideas and issues, not people.The Democratic Party has for years taken Blacks for granted."

"My lady friend Josephine is a registered Republican."

Diana responded, "That doesn't bother you?"

"Of course not! We usually agree on issues and vote the same way. She tells me whatthe Republicans are thinking and I tell her what the Democrats are thinking."

"My parents always voted for the Democrats. They grew up during the civil rightsmovement. Blacks and whites did not attend church together even though theybelonged to the same denomination and worshiped the same God."

"During this time in our history, Blacks got paid less for doing the same type of work, and worse than that, Blacks were excluded from certain types of jobs."

"They couldn't work in banks, serve people in white only restaurants, work as cashiersin supermarkets, teach white children in the public school system, buy land or housesin certain neighborhoods, buy new cars from some dealers and couldn't even walk on theside-walk if a white person was coming."

"I can't imagine living that way," Diana said. "Are you bitter Mr. Carter?"

"No!" I replied. "My parents and grandparents lived through that, not me. When I wasborn, things had improved. Most of what I know came from conversations with myparents, movies and from a few books I have read."

"I had a pastor who participated in the Baton Rouge bus boycott."

"Diana, why don't you go to the county library and check out some books on the civilrights movement. It'll make you a better congresswoman."

"That should be interesting," Diana uttered.Suddenly I felt a pair of small, soft hands around my neck. Before I could react, Dianapressed her lips against my right cheek. She then moved backwards and sat back on theseat.

"Thanks Mr. Carter."

"You're welcome."

The kiss on the cheek was innocent and I wasn't going to worry about it. I felt proudthat I had been successful in teaching this student a new course.

Leaning forward again, Diana said, "I think I'm going to marry a Black man."

Now I wondered had my conversation been misunderstood.

"Why would you want to marry a Black man?" I asked.

Diana responded with, "I think it would make life more interesting."

I turned sideways in the seat, turned the volume down on the tape that was playing,looked Diana straight in the eyes and said, "The color of a man's skin is not going tomake life interesting. An interesting man will make life interesting."

Diana answered, "When I'm twenty-one, you will be in your early thirties. Then I canmarry you."

"I don't think I'm going to wait that long. I'll probably get married in two or threeyears," I replied.

"To that Josephine person I assume?"

"Yes," I responded.

As the cassette completed it's last song, I turned the tape off and turned the radio backon. There were several twenty-four hour stations that played good music all night. I alsowanted to hear any updates on the earthquake.

Diana got up and moved to the back seat. I sensed that the conversation was over. AsI turned the volume up on the radio, I could hear the girls laughing as they approachedthe van.

"Here they come," remarked Diana in a sarcastic tone, as though her privacy was aboutto be invaded.

I was getting tired and sleepy. I also needed to empty my bladder. I opened the door,got out and walked to the front of the van. As the girls passed by, Cheryl said the waterhad gone down some and you could see where some of the road had been washed away.I told the girls to get back into the van and try to get some rest or some sleep. Patriciasaid she was too hungry to sleep.

I remembered she didn't eat as much as the others. She only ate a salad.

I told the girls that I would be right back. I headed for the edge of the cliff. I stoppedbehind one of the larger trees, looked back at the van to make sure all the girls were stillinside. I unzipped my pants, pulled out Junior, (That's what Josephine calls it) and started urinating. The urine came slowly, as Junior was harder than normal. SuddenlyI heard the van door close. Just as I concluded peeing, Patricia walked up. Iimmediately walked away from the freshly watered tree, not wanting Patricia to knowwhat I had been doing. Plus I had passed gas a couple of times, and even to me thesefarts were extremely offensive.

Patricia was older and larger than the other girls. She was twelve. Her parents movedaround the country a lot when she was younger and that caused her to be retained in thesame grade one year. Her father was unable to keep a job very long because of hisdrinking.

Patricia followed closely behind, not saying anything.

When I believed that I had reached a safe distance from the foul smelling air, I turnedand faced Patricia.

"Patricia, I thought I told you to get some sleep!"

"I'm not sleepy" she responded. "I know you were empting your bladder."

"That's right," I responded. I started thinking about how these children talk. Backhome no one would say, "Empty your bladder." It would have been, "Taking a leak."

Patricia's facial expression then changed from distant to a more serious expression.She then walked closer to the edge of the cliff away from me.

"Mr. Carter, there's this boy at school who asked me to have sex with him. He's in the eighth grade."

"What did you tell him?" I asked.

"I told him I would think about it."

"Patricia, you are too young. You have plenty of time ahead of you to have sex. Waita few years. You need to experience love first.

Patricia, this is something you need todiscuss with your mother."

I waited for a response from Patricia. She then picked up a hand full of the pebbles andtossed them at a nearby tree.

"My mother can't help me."

"Yes she can. She can prepare you for when the time does come or when the time isright."

"What do you mean prepare me?"

"Patricia, sometimes a man will have sex with a woman for the first time, and then hewon't speak to her after that. Then the woman's heart is broken and she becomesangry or disappointed. In addition to the emotional letdowns that can occur, there's thepossibility of disease or pregnancy."

"Mr. Carter, I know all that stuff. Plus he said he was going to use a condom."

"Pat, you still need to wait until you're older. Also, as I said before, you need todiscuss this with your mother. Your mother has years of knowledge and experiences that would benefit you and help you understand the situation better."

At that moment, I thought the conversation was over. Pat turned and started walking slowly toward the van. Suddenly she turned back around and said, "Last weekBruce kissed me."

I really didn't want to know the guy's name.

Patricia, seemingly deep in thought and a little too close to me, said, "I kissed himback. While we were kissing, he started rubbing my breast and then he startedsqueezing my butt."

She was apparently reliving the moment in her mind as she held her breast in her handand softly stroked it as she described her experience.

Then I asked, "What else happened?" I was thinking that Bruce may have violated herand she needed to tell somebody.

"I pulled away. He grabbed me and pulled me back. It felt good. That's when he askedme to have sex with him."

"Did he do anything else?"

"After I told him I would think about it, he kissed me again and put his hand on myother breast. He then took my hand from off his shoulder and brought it down to hiscock. I squeezed it a couple of times. Then I took my arm from around him and backedup."

"Mr. Carter, I wanted to do it so badly. That's all I have been thinking about."

As I looked at Pat's silhouette in the moonlight, I saw a twelve year old with tightfitting shorts on and a long sleeve tight fitting blouse. She was as large and curvy assome women twice her age. She had very shapely legs, a small waistline, big hips anda bosom far beyond her age. She could match Josephine part by part except Josephine was a few inches taller. I could see why this guy wanted to have sex withher.

Sometimes during the conversation, Junior had escaped and was standing at attention.Pat was staring in that direction. The moonlight gave just enough light so she couldsee the bulge in my pants. As she looked up, I put my left hand in my pocket andattempted to make an adjustment.

Pat then uttered, "You have probably thought about having sex with me too, haven'tyou?"

My first thought was to get her back to the van as quickly as possible. But I thought itwould be best if I could first get these thoughts out of her head.

"Pat, I only want to have sex with women my age, not with twelve year old girls.Plus, as school teachers we are prohibited from having any personal relationships with ourstudents. It would cost us our job."

"It is against the law for someone of your age to get involved in sexual activities. If youare caught, you can get the boy in trouble as well as your parents. You have told mestories about how good your stepfather has been to you and your family. I think he would be very disappointed in you if you did something wrong."

Her facial expression changed. I wasn't sure if it was a look of disappointment or thelook of someone who had just been insulted.

She took two steps toward me. She had a look on her face that said what I had just saidto her had no meaning. She seemed to have been positioning herself for a kiss from me.

I moved quickly from my position before she could make contact with me. I grabbedher by her right arm, turned her around with her back at my front, and using someforce, starting her moving in the direction of the van.

Pat said nothing. She leaned backward. Using my strength, with one hand on hershoulder, I continued to push her toward the van. After getting within fifteen yards of thevan, I released my grip from her arm and shoulder. I stopped and waited for her toproceed on her on. She paused for a moment. Then with one motion, she took offtoward the van while swinging one of her hands backward, landing it directly in themiddle of my crouch. Pat entered the van and went straight to the back seat, which ofcourse is the farthest from the driver's seat.

Before I opened the door to the van, I took a deep breath. The inside of my body wasracing with feelings that were similar to those feelings I get when I'm with Josephine.

Most men have probably dreamed of being stranded on an island with some beautifulwomen. Here I am stuck in the woods with five fifth grade students.

It would be easier with boys in this situation. I finally opened the door to the van, but did not get in. Everyone appeared to be sleep or was trying to go to sleep.Music was still coming from the radio with the volume turned down real low. Onthe second seat, Diana and Myrisha appeared to be sleep. Pat had joined Cheryl on theback seat. Kim was again in the front passenger seat. She was not asleep. She wasstaring at me with those big blue eyes.

I closed the door to the van putting the girls in the dark. The moon was beginning tofade behind the trees at the edge of the cliff reducing the amount of light it hadpreviously been providing. As I stood leaning against the van, I could feel the groundshaking again. This was another aftershock. More rocks fell. However, what fell thistime only amounted to a trickle.

The road behind us continued to wash away, but at a much slower pace. The worstseemed to have passed.

As I continued to lean against the van, I began to reminisce about the conversationsand actions of Kim, Diana and Patricia. I was thinking about how fine Pat is. I couldprobably understand why Bruce was trying to get into her pants.

As I climbed back into the van, my thoughts focused back to my college days. Oneparticular cheerleader with a Coca-Cola bottle figure came to mind. She was so fine,I would attend home basketball games just to see her dance. This girl was a freshmanwhen she started cheering, and was the finest chick on campus. After basketball season,I did not see her again that year.

When she came back to campus as a sophomore, she had gained about twenty pounds.One of her homeboys told me that she had an older sister who was fine just like thatwhen she was at that age. But her sister was pushing two hundred and fifty pounds bythe time she was thirty years old. The cheerleader was enrolled in a two-year course andleft school and the area after her sophomore year. But I was told later that she wasfollowing in her sister's footsteps.

I guess I thought of that because of Pat. I have seen Pat's mother. She has a well-shaped body, but must be tipping the scale around two-hundred and fifty pounds.

I started trying to imagine what these girls would look like in fifteen years. Will Pat befat?" Will Diana become a doctor or be involved in politics?" Will Kim be as pretty asshe is now?

An old favorite song of mine interrupted my thought process. It was a song by BobDylan titled, "Everybody's Got to Serve Somebody."

Cheryl and Pat were whispering in the back and Kim was still watching me. As soon asthe song was over, I asked Kim if there had been any updates on the earthquake while Iwas out of the van.

Kim replied, "There was a lot of damage in the Burbank area. They didn't mentionanything about an old man and five ladies missing."

Pat didn't say anything, but Cheryl laughed.

After listening to Cheryl laugh for longer than necessary, I started feeling the hunger pains coming from my stomach. I had a pack of Mentos in my console and three slices ofBig Red gum.

I offered the girls some of my Mentos. I told them that they could have two each andthat I would save some for Myrisha and Diana.

After a few commercials, the radio station kicked off with a country song by RickySkaggs. I wasn't familiar with the song.

Cheryl asked if she could change the station.

I told her, "No."

Cheryl said, "Mr. Carter, I don't like that kind of music."

"Cheryl, go to sleep," I replied.

After a pause, Cheryl said, "If Kimberly wanted to change the station you would have lether."

Kim smiled, looked back at Cheryl and said, "That's right."

While reaching for the radio dial, Kim turned to me and said, "Wendell, is it okay if I

change the station?"

Before I could answer, Cheryl and Pat in concert, Wendell?"

"Are ya'll on a first name basis?" asked Cheryl.

"She's just being an ass, "Pat added.

I reached for the radio-tuning knob. Kim's hand had beaten mine to that destination.As I attempted to turn the knob to the right, Kim tried to turn it to the left. I removed my hand after realizing that she seemed to be getting some pleasure from my touch. Shefound a station playing some pop music. A new release from Brittany Spears came onthe radio.

Cheryl again, with a begging voice, said, "Find something else on the radio. I don'twant to hear that white music Mr. Carter."

Pat responded, "What is white music?"

"The kind of music that's on the radio," responded Cheryl.

She continued, "This is Mr. Carter's van and he's a brother, so we should be listeningto soul music. I know Mr. Carter don't want to hear Brittany Spears."

Diana responded, "I like soul music."

"Kimberly intervened, "Diana, stop kissing up to Cheryl. There are four of us to one ofher, so we should have the right to listen to the type of music that we want to."

"Girl you better stop playing with me. The way I feel right now, I'll beat your butt,"Cheryl said.

Kimberly, turning around and kneeling in the seat, her face minus the constant smile thatseemingly always accompany her, pointed to Cheryl and said, "I'm not afraid of you."

Cheryl responded, "I'm not afraid of you either pretty girl. If you want some of this,we can go outside."

Kimberly slipped her shoes on. Then turned to Cheryl and said, "Let's go. We can getthis over with right now."

Kimberly turned and opened the front door. Cheryl stood up and crossed over Pat andstarted leaving the back seat.

Before I could act or say anything, the van started shaking again. We had justexperienced another aftershock.

Kimberly paused, sat back down and then closed the door. Cheryl slowly retreatedback to her seat.

We all sat in silence and listened to the rumbling as the van bounced ever so slowlybeneath us. The words exchanged between Cheryl and Kimberly seemed to be a thingof the past.

With the landscape being darkened by the descending moon, it had become increasinglyharder to see what was happening outside. I turned my headlights on and saw nothingdifferent in front of us.

I exited the van and looked to the rear. A part of the roadway which had been supportingthe makeshift waterfall had clasped and was sliding into the valley. Our football fieldbegan to look more like a basketball court as our safe haven became smaller and smaller.

The girls knew that this was no longer the overnight camping trip that they were soanxious to tell their family and friends about, but a real dangerous and scary situation.

I got back into the van. The piece of land we were parked on felt solid. No waterhad flowed over this section

On entering the van, I could hear a sobbing noise coming from the back.

"Mr. Carter, Patricia is crying," remarked Diana.

"What's wrong Patricia?"

"I'm scared. I don't want to die out here. I want my family."

I remembered that Patricia's dad had died in a car crash. She was probably thinking about her father.

"I just miss my family. I've never been away from home overnight before."

"Myrisha uttered, "It's no big deal. I've stayed in a hotel room all night by myself inLas Vegas."

Cheryl put her arm around Patricia and pulled her to her shoulder. Patricia'swhimpering sound could not overcome the growling sound coming from her stomach,which reminded all of us that there had been no dinner last night.I reassured the girls that we were safe and that everything would be okay.After a few minutes of calm, I told the girls that I was going to take a walk and for themnot to leave the van. My eyes were getting heavy. The Mentos didn't do much goodhelping me stay awake. I didn't think it would be wise for me to fall asleep.

I walked toward the rocks that had fallen in front of us. I was thinking how I hadwasted a good weekend night. I checked my watch. It was after two. As I continuedwalking, I heard the van door open and close. I saw Kim and Myrisha headed for thetrees. I yelled and told them to be careful and not to go beyond a certain point. At thesame time, Cheryl was approaching me.

I asked her if the other two were going urinate.

Cheryl laughed and then replied, "No, they are going pee."

"Don't you want to go pee," I asked her.

She said yes and then pulled her pants down about six inches as though she was goingto do it in front of me.

She laughed. "You know I wouldn't do that in front of you Wendell!"

"I hope not," I responded. "Go get some sleep."

Cheryl then asked, "Mr. Carter, do you have feelings for Kimberly?"

"Of course not," I answered. Then I asked her to tell me exactly what did she mean. Itold her that I have feelings for all of my students.

"Kimberly just told us that you had a crush on her. I know you don't like that white girlbetter than me."

"Of course not," I replied.

"Cheryl, I don't decide how much I like someone based on the color of their skin.Cheryl, I believe loving someone or caring for someone is more about what you feel, notwhat you see. Lil' sister, there are going to be times when we are going to be broughttogether because of the color of our skin, and the others will be on the opposite side. Butas a teacher, I have to try to treat all of my students the same, whether they are black,red or white: Whether they are male or female; or whether they are brilliant or slow."

"Cheryl, I'm going to tell you a story. When I was in the eighth grade, I met a girl with some big pretty brown eyes and a million dollar smile. She was cute and had a well-shaped body. She was the bomb! When I found out that she was interested in me, itblew my mind."

"When I met her, I already had a girlfriend whom I broke up with immediately. Forthe next two weeks, this girl and I spent hours and hours together parading around thecampus everyday. I was walking around with my chest poked out knowing that manyof my friends wished they were in my shoes."

"Then one Sunday, I couldn't see her because I had to play baseball. But the game wascancelled. I got on my bicycle and headed to her house. About three blocks from herhouse, I saw her walking down the street hugged up with another guy who was a coupleof years older than me."

"I turned and headed home. Seeing her with another guy didn't hurt because I realizedthat I did not love her. I was only interested in her looks and her body. Since that day, Ihave vowed to never fall for a woman just because of the way she looks. It doesn'tmatter if she is fine, cute, rich, white or yellow. It's what's inside that counts. I alwaysstart with a nice personality and then go from there. Even Josephine had to go throughthe personality and intelligence tests. When I met Josephine, I didn't know anything abouther, but she made a good first impression."

Cheryl, after listening patiently and attentively, said, "If you had to choose between us,then you would probably choose me, because I know I have a better personality than those white girls."

After that remark, I decided to try a different angle.

"Sure," I said. "I would definitely choose you."

Cheryl smiled. "You must think I'm stupid," she responded.

"Okay, then no. I would not choose you."

Cheryl then asked, "Do all men lie? My daddy is always lying to my mother. Ialways hear my mother telling my dad that he is lying, especially when he comes inlate from work. He always tells her that he was at some bar."

"How does she know he wasn't? He is a musician," I remarked.

Cheryl took a few steps toward the blocked road with her mood changing fromhumorous to serious.

As she turned and faced me again, she said she overheard her daddy talking to a friendon the telephone one day. She said he was complaining about her mother not wanting tohave sex often enough and that he had gotten tired of begging and fighting. He said thatis why he does what he does.

"At that point, I eased out of the room. I didn't want to hear any-more, "Cherylcontinued.

"Did you talk to your dad about it?"

"No."

"Did you tell your mother?"

Cheryl said, "I wanted to but I was afraid that if I told her it might cause my parents todivorce."

This wasn't anything I hadn't heard before. I knew this problem existed in some waybetween my parents. I remember watching Dr.

49

Phil discussing problems with couples nothaving enough sex in their marriages on the Oprah show one day.

"Cheryl, that is something you shouldn't worry about. If your parents love each other,their marriage will survive," I explained. "I don't know exactly what the answer is, butas women grow older, their attention turns more to raising a family, taking care of theirhomes and working at their careers. Sex sort of slips down the list of priorities.""Men on the other hand, have a sex drive that does not level off as soon as mostwomen, "I continued. "Many of them will find sex elsewhere if they can't get it at home.But a man has to be careful because he doesn't want to bring a disease home to his wifeor get involved with a crazy woman?"

"What's a crazy woman?"

"It's a woman who will call a man's house, cut the tires on his car, or create a scene ina place when she knows it will cause problems between him and his family."

"Then sometimes Cheryl. men will actually leave their wives and families for anotherwoman. Sometimes that other woman is so much better than what he has at home that hecan't resist leaving."

I continued to lecture Cheryl about marriage. I got to a point where I believed I was trying to cover all bases. Subconsciously, I was thinking about her father. I have seen himin various clubs around town, and he was usually with some chick. He is a good musician.He and a couple of his old fraternity brothers are always partying with the ladies after hefinishes playing music. In addition to everything else, he drives a convertible sports car.

He has never come to the school and doesn't know me. One night while visiting a clubhe was performing at, I caught him staring at Josephine. I wouldn't be shocked orsurprised if he deserted Cheryl's mother. I've seen him with some honeys that lookedbetter than Josephine. Of course, I couldn't tell if they had anything else going for thembesides their looks.

I put my hand around Cheryl's shoulder as I guided her in the direction of the van. Icontinued my conversation.

"Cheryl, sometimes couples grow apart, especially when they get married young. Oneof the parties will improve or change for the better and the other will remain the same.This is called growing apart."

"Another problem, sometimes one of the partners changes physically. A man maybecome bald, or a lady may become overweight. Sometimes one of the partners maystart drinking too much or get hooked on drugs. Cheryl, even getting involved with toomany organizations or hobbies can be a problem, especially if the partner is not involvedin any."

"Not only should couples respect each other, but they should be friends."

"But one of the basic strengths of a marriage is that both parties have enough incommon so that they can spend time doing things together that they both enjoy."

Cheryl asked, "Do you and Josephine have a lot in common?"

"Yes we do," I replied. "But we are not married."

As we approached the van, I could see that the other four girls were in the vehicle.Cheryl wanted to know how I met Josephine. She turned her back toward the van.My hand slid off of her shoulder. Her arm came from around my waist, which Ihadn't realized was there. She asked again, seeming to be real interested in Josephineand me.

"The first time I saw Josephine, I had gone to New Orleans for rehearsal for a wedding.I didn't know if she was the bride or one of the maids. I couldn't keep my eyes off ofher. Finally, this lady told us to line up. All the guys had to go to the left side of thechurch and all the girls went to the back. The lady told me to get fifth in line, whichwould make me march just ahead of the best man."

"As the ladies started marching in, I noticed that Josephine was fifth. When it was timefor me to march, I saw Josephine coming toward me. Having never been introduced,when we met, I told her my name and that I was single. She said she was married andhad six children. I told her, 'Yes I know. Your husband told me just before hecommitted suicide.'"

"Josephine laughed. I could sense a good sense of humor and a good personality, two things that I loved in a lady. Plus she was very attractive."

"After practice, I asked her out to dinner. She accepted and took me across the streetto a Burger King."

"We really clicked. We talked for three hours. During that time, we exchangedaddresses and phone numbers. The wedding was the next day."

"Following the wedding, she agreed to go to Thibodaux with me to visit Nicholls StateUniversity. During our visit, there was a point when we looked at each other and justembraced and kissed. I had never met a girl like Josephine before."

"During our drive back to New Orleans that night, she indicated that she would bemoving back to California after graduation. She had worked at a motel the last twosummers and the company of-fered her a permanent job in management when she finishedcollege. She accepted the job, but it was in the Los Angeles area."

"During the next few months, we spent as much time together as possible. Duringthose months, we discovered that we enjoyed doing many different things together, andhad many of the same interest."

"One night I took her to a baseball game in New Orleans. Her roommate at Dillardsaid Josephine didn't like baseball. Josephine said she didn't know if she liked baseballor not. She had never seen a baseball game before. But she said she would enjoy herselfwherever she went, as long as she was with me. It's the same way with me. I enjoymyself every time I'm with her, and it doesn't matter what the occasion is."

"What we have is rare. Your parents may not have the chemistry that I have withJosephine, but they are probably still a good couple in love. I wouldn't worry about yourmother and father. I think just having a daughter like you is enough to keep themtogether."

As I was concluding my conversation with Cheryl, the door to the van opened.Myrisha stepped out onto the ground. She stood with her back leaning against the van.

"Mr. Carter, I need to tell Cheryl something. Could you please excuse us?"

"Sure," I replied.

Then I walked to the driver's side of the van and got in.

At the same time, Myrisha and Cheryl started walking toward the back of the van. Thetwo of them conversed for a short while before Cheryl came back and got into the van.She grabbed her tote and Myrisha's bags. She exited the van again. The two girlsheaded toward the trees near the edge of the cliff. I had no idea what was going on.

Suddenly, I could hear a snore coming from the back seat. Patricia had fallen asleepand was snoring a little. Both Kimberly and Diana had their heads leaning on the windowsnext to them. They were either sleep or resting their eyes.

After a few minutes, I could see Cheryl and Myrisha returning to the van. Myrisha hadchanged clothes. She had changed into one of the outfits she purchased from the gift shopwhen we were at the cavern.

As the two girls got into the van, both were completely silent. Myrisha was taking more time to get settled than normally. Eventually, she sat down, but with a couple ofclothing items beneath her. I assumed she was trying to set on something a little softerthan my seat.

"What's wrong? My seat isn't soft enough for you?"

Myrisha didn't answer. She just stared at me briefly and then turned her head towardthe outer window. After a few moments of silence, Myrisha broke the ice.

She leaned over the back of my seat and whispered into my ear, "Wendell, I'm awoman now."

Not sure what she meant, I just remained silent.

After a few minutes passed, Myrisha leaned over the back of my seat again andwhispered into my ear, "I had my first period."

All of a sudden my sense of smell seemed to have been activated. The odor comingfrom Myrisha was not only French perfume, which she likes to wear, but what I detectedwas a mixture of not bathing for almost twenty-four hours and whatever an eleven yearold's menstrual cycle smells like.

Not sure what to say to Myrisha, I could sense she was fishing for some type ofcomment from me, so I just said, "Congratulations Myrisha."

"Thanks Wendell," she replied

"You're welcome," Myrisha.

Cheryl could be heard yawning in the background.

My thoughts turned to my seat where Myrisha had placed the clothing she was sittingon. Maybe it was not a mater of comfort, but one of blood. I was hoping she had notstained my seat too badly. I was afraid to ask.

The next few minutes were quiet ones. I yawned over and over again as I fought goingto sleep. I thought all of the girls were asleep at this time. Suddenly, I heard whatsounded like paper. When I looked back, Myrisha was counting money.

"Myrisha, how much money did you bring with you?"

"I brought three-hundred dollars."

"That's a lot of money to bring on a field trip," I exclaimed.

"My mother gives me fifty dollars a week for my allowance and I can spend it any wayI want to."

"You're lucky that your parents can provide you with that kind of security," I replied.

Myrisha asked, "How much allowance did your parents give you?"

"Allowance? My parents never could afford to give my sisters and me any allowance.They needed every penny just to feed us and keep a roof over our heads."

"How did you get through college, "Myrisha asked.

"I had to work in high school and the entire time I spent in college," I replied.

Myrisha asked, "Where did you go to college?"

"I got my bachelors degree from Nicholls State University in Thibodaux, La."

"Is that near the French Quarter?" Myrisha asked.

"No," I replied. "The French Quarter is in New Orleans which is about sixty milesfrom Thibodaux."

As I looked around the van, the other four girls were asleep. Myrisha was probablybeing kept awake by the adrenaline flowing through her veins as the result ofexperiencing her first period.

"I want to go to New Orleans and the South one day," Myrisha said. "My parentsalways take me to Colorado to ski or to Hawaii. They don't take me with them whenthey go to Las Vegas anymore."

Myrisha continued; "I told my mother that I wanted to go to a college in the South andshe told me that I had to go to U. C. L. A. because she went there."

"The South is a big place. Do you have any idea what colleges or state you might beinteresting in?"

"I always hear a lot about Alabama, L. S. U. and Georgia. The college I go to has to bein a city that has a good mall. My dad wants me to go to an Ivy League school."

"Ivy League?" As I thought to myself, Myrisha has a C average. I wonder how herfather expects to get her into an Ivy league school. I don't think they would enroll herbased on her father's money. Plus, that is a long ways from home. I am surprised hedidn't mention Stanford.

Diana, with her straight A average could get into an Ivy League school. Perhaps Kim and Cheryl could get in also. Myrisha apparently does not understand how importantgrades are as they relate to enrolling into college.

"Myrisha, you have a lot of time to decide where you are going to attend college. Youshould be thinking about junior high school, or at least high school and not about collegealready," I exclaimed. "You may not want to go to college when you finish high school.You might decide to go to a vocational school or to some type of specialty training school. You may also want to join the military."

"Military! I'm not a lesbian," shouted Myrisha.

"You do not have to be a lesbian to go to the military."

As I continued to yawn and fight sleep, I told Myrisha to get some sleep and that wewould continue our conversation at a later date.

"Myrisha, you have plenty of time to think about those things. Heck, you're just ababy."

Maybe it was the sleepiness that had come upon me that caused me to use the wordbaby, but Myrisha didn't like that at all.

Myrisha leaned over the back of my seat and got real close to me. My first thought wasthat she was going to kiss me on the cheek and tell me good night or good morning.

"Baby! I'm no goddamn baby Wendell."

Myrisha must have spoken loud enough for Cheryl to hear her from the back seat.Cheryl laughed and told Myrisha not to get carried away.

"I'm as much woman as some of those teachers at school," Myrisha uttered.Myrisha then asked Cheryl to switch seats. My back seats folded down. Pat andCheryl had been lying down. Kim had the passenger seat fully reclined. Only Diana andMyrisha were forced to sit or sleep in an upright position. When Cheryl refused toswitch seats, Myrisha pulled out a twenty-dollar bill and reached to Cheryl. Cheryl askedfor forty. Pat, awakened sometimes during the on-going activities, grabbed the twentyand told Myrisha to take her seat.

Pat and Myrisha switched seats. Pat sat on the shirts Myrisha had placed on the seat.She rose up and removed the shirts and handed them back to Myrisha.

Cheryl was on the back seat begging Myrisha for twenty-dollars.

I turned around and looked at Cheryl. Myrisha had put her money away and stretchedout on the back seat.

"Cheryl, stop begging. You had a chance to get twenty dollars and you got greedy," Isaid to her.

Myrisha reached into her purse and pulled out a twenty and handed it to Cheryl.Suddenly Kim sat up and asked Myrisha for hers. Myrisha gave Kim a twenty and thenfolded one up and stuck it in Diana's pocket.

"Wait a minute! That's not fair," uttered Pat. "I gave you my seat for my twenty-dollarsand they didn't do anything. I should get more money than them."

Myrisha closed her purse and laid back down.

"Hold up," I said. "Give me all of the money. No one is going to sell seats in my van."

"No one is buying or selling seats," yelled Myrisha. "I'm just being nice to myfriends."

"If you don't give them any money, then they won't be your friends."

"Yes they will be my friends," replied Myrisha. "And if I want to give them money,that's my business and you don't have anything to do with it." "As long as you're on this field trip and riding in my van, I will have something to sayabout it Miss Smarty."

None of the girls had parted with the money that Myrisha had given them.

Myrisha again addressed me as Wendell, saying that she didn't have to buy friendshipbecause everyone liked her because of her personality.

"I guess it's natural for people like you to use money for any situation," I said.

"My mother says that money can open doors and influence people. She said if youhave money, you can help people who have less than you." continued Myrisha. "You'reprobably just mad because I didn't give you any. I know men like money too, and mymother says that school teachers don't make that much money anyway."

Diana had joined the listeners as they turned from me to Myrisha waiting on the nextcomment as though they were watching a tennis match.

Myrisha said, "My mother told me that all men liked was money, sex and sports. I know you like sports because I see you playing basketball all the time; and I know youlike women because I see that whore dropping you off at school sometimes; and I knowyou like money because everybody likes money."

57

"Mr. Carter, she called Josephine a whore," remarked Kimberly.

"He's just talking like that because you girls are here. If you weren't here, Mr. Carterwould be all over me for my money," Myrisha replied.

"Myrisha, no one wants to be all over you, especially right now. Did you forget whathappened earlier?" Cheryl said.

"What happened earlier?" Diana asked.

"Girl, Myrisha had her first period," exclaimed Cheryl.

Pat immediately jumped up from her seat, knowing that she was sitting on the seatwhere Myrisha had been sitting and where she had the shirts. She opened the door toallow the overhead light to come on. Pat focused her eyes on the seat where she had beensitting. She turned and asked Diana if she had any blood on the back of her pants. Dianatold her no. While they were looking, so was I. There appeared to be a little stain on theseat about the size of a quarter.

I wasn't too happy about that. My van was not new when I bought it, but it was veryclean. The second and third seats had rarely been used. I bought the van from a dealershipin New Orleans after an old couple used it for a couple of years and then traded it in.The dealership called it a certified vehicle. It wasn't what I wanted but it was what I needed. It was inexpensive and roomy enough for me to load and carry nearly all of mybelongings with me when I moved to California.

Before sitting back down, Pat reached into her tote and took out what looked like asouvenir brochure. She opened it, placed it on the seat, and then sat back down.

"Oh Myrisha, you're going to give that stuff away now," Pat said.

"Nobody's going to want that unless she pays them," uttered Kimberly.

"Screw both of you," Myrisha replied. "I don't have to buy anybody. I can getanybody I want with my looks and personality."

The girls gave no response to that comment by Myrisha.

Myrisha continued, "My mother said that boys are going to want me because of mymoney."

"You mean your parents money, don't you?" remarked Kimberly.

Myrisha then revealed that she receives an allowance of fifty-dollars a week, pluson her birthday and for Christmas, she receives five hundred dollars.

None of the girls had raised a hand to return any of the money that Myrisha had giventhem earlier. I believe they had just ignored me when I asked them to return it.

Anyway, Kimberly asked Myrisha what did she do with all of her money.

She said she spends most of it in the mall, but her mother requires her to save a portionof it every month.

"I know you get a big discount when you shop at your mother's store," Kimberlycontinued.

"It's not a store, it's a boutique," snapped Myrisha. "I don't buy clothes from mymother's boutique. I just tell her what I like in the boutique and she buys it and bringsit home."

"Let's leave Myrisha alone," uttered Cheryl. "After all, she did give us that money.That means we are friends." After laughing momentarily, Cheryl continued, speakingin a voice mocking a slave, "We is your girls Miss Myrisha and we doesn't want tomake you mad."

The girls laughed.

"All of you can kiss my ass," yelled Myrisha.

I was beginning to feel sorry for Myrisha, but I thought it was better for me not to getinvolved. Daylight was approaching and I was still fighting sleep.

After absorbing what Myrisha had just said, Cheryl told Myrisha if she was going totalk to her that way, she would take her sanitary napkin back.

Myrisha stood up, reached inside her shorts and quickly flung her hand toward Cheryl.Cheryl screamed and ducked as though she wasn't sure if Myrisha was indeed returningher sanitary napkin.

Diana then said, "The two of you are too filthy."

A few moments of silence ensued, then Pat started another discussion.

Pat followed with the same revelation to the girls that she had revealed to me earlier inthe morning that Bruce and some other guys were trying to get her to have sex with them.

Cheryl said, "You may as well go ahead and give it to them because you're going to bea whore anyway."

"Just because I'm fine, that doesn't mean I have to be a whore, bitch," Pat responded.

"You didn't get that way without some help from somebody, whore," Cheryl replied.

"Your mama is a whore," remarked Pat.

"Don't you talk about my mama. I'll beat your ass!" declared Cheryl.

With tension building between the two girls, I thought I was going to have to break up afight.

Kimberly intervened however and said, "Neither one of you are worth a damn, so whydon't you go jump off the cliff over there (Kim, pointing in the direction of the cliff)."

"Who asked you for your two cents pretty girl," Pat said. "All you've been doing all morning is sucking up to that man up there. Every time I look, you're staring in hisface."

Cheryl said, "I agree. Wendell don't want you pretty girl. The soul brother likes sisterslike Josephine and me. So you can stop twisting your little ass around up there."

"You are just jealous," remarked Kimberly.

Pat then stood up and turned her adult ass to Kim, rubbing it with a circular motion andsaid, "Wendell will take this any day before he gets excited over your little blue eyes and flat ass."

While all the talking was going on, Myrisha and Diana were watching and listening.Diana would smile at some of the comments, but her mood was not as jovial as the othergirls. Kim noticed that Diana was staring at her with a smile following the last remarkand demonstration by Pat.

"Do you have anything to say?" Kim asked Diana.

"No!" responded Diana. "I'm just listening and learning."

"Diana, you need to take your head out off those books sometimes and learn what'sgoing on in the real world," remarked Cheryl.

Diana replied, "I don't just read school books. I read all kinds of books. I have evenread books about your people Cheryl."

"My people! What in the hell so you mean by my people?"

Before Diana could answer, Pat yelled out, "Jungle bunnies."

Cheryl just laughed at the remark by Pat. Cheryl then told Pat that she wouldremember that when she see her working on the strip.

"I'm not going to be on the street. I'm going to work out of the presidential suite at thePlaza," Pat said. "Diana is going to be on the strip reading to the prostitutes and thepimps."

Pat asked, "Diana, have you read what a prostitute is yet?"

"Yes I have," Diana remarked. "And when I get elected to the leg-islature, I'm going to pass some laws to put them out of business."

Cheryl said, "Girl, as soon as some man burst your cherry, you are going to forget allabout some legislature. You're going to be out there on the strip with Pat selling booty."

The other three girls laughed. Diana looked back at Cheryl and rolled her eyes.I continued to remain quiet, content that I had been left completely out of the recentconversations between the girls. I sat with my eyes closed while listening to all the surprising remarks coming from my valley girls. But I have to admit, Junior got excit-edsomewhere during these conversations. I had my hand resting on Junior and wondered ifKim was looking.

Suddenly, I heard Myrisha and Kimberly yawning. Kimberly had the seat reclined withher feet resting on the dashboard.

Kimberly was very hairy. I started imagining her being older and playing with Juniorwhile I stroked her legs. Then my thoughts would wander to Pat. I pictured her sittingon my lap while I stroked her breast. But my thought pattern seems to be totally differentfor the other three girls. I was visualizing Diana as a well respected commu-nity leader asI accompanied her to the governor's ball with Myrisha's company catering the ball.Myrisha was married to a senator. I saw Cheryl at the ball too. She was receiving anaward for being the states outstanding female athlete. Suddenly, the governor wasintroduced along with his beautiful wife, Kimberly. Later during the ball Diana wanted to spend some time with some of her friends. On my way to the restroom, Patricia pulledme into a room and told me she wanted to make love to me. I immediately obliged. Iwas imagining having sex with Patricia, but it was the same Patricia in my van and not anadult version. My mind stopped wondering when I realized that Junior was not only hard,but also full. I needed to go urinate again.

I sat up, rubbed my eyes, and then opened the door. I told the girls that I would be rightback. I thought it would be better now than after daylight.

As I departed the van, Kim said something that I thought would have come from Pat orCheryl, the two who seemed to be the more outspoken.

I could hear Kimberly telling the others, "Wendell is going masturbate."

I could hear the girls chuckling. As I moved further away from the van, the soundsfaded. I went behind a tree and urinated. When I finished, I walked to the edge of thecliff and looked down into the valley. It was more visible now than it was the last time Ihad been here. The air was still a little cool. A light breeze was blowing to make it evenchillier. But the fresh air was a welcomed relief from the stuffy air in the van. I tookseveral deep breaths, so as to fill my lungs with fresh air.

When we left school yesterday, the girls smelled so good, especially Myrisha with herhigh priced perfume. But a lot had changed since then. I never imagined these girls couldsmell so strong, especially Myrisha with her new found womanhood.

As I started back toward the van, I saw four of the girls coming toward me. As they drew closer, Kimberly said, "We are going pee."

Myrisha was not with them, but still in the van.

I arrived at the van, opened the door and got in. Myrisha had moved to the frontpassenger seat and was tuning the radio. The radio had been off for a couple of hours. Iturned the key in the ignition from the auxiliary position and started the engine. I turnedthe vent on and opened the windows to circulate some fresh air throughout the van.

'Wendell, do I smell that bad?" Myrisha asked.

"Yes," I replied.

Knowing that we were alone, I guess this gave Myrisha an opportunity to put me to thetest.

After settling on a radio station playing some pop music, she then pulled her shirt upand removed her training bra. I looked and wondered what she was going to do next.She made sure I got a chance to see the little nubs on her chest. She pulled her shirtdown and put her bra in her bag.

"Now that I'm a woman, do you think they will grow bigger?" Myrisha asked.

"Yes Myrisha. They will grow larger."

She had a smile of contentment on her face, probably thinking about how she wasgoing to use them in the future. She was shifting in the front seat, going from beingballed up in a knot to wiggling.

I asked her if she had to use the bathroom.

She laughed and said that there was no bathroom out here. She said that she didn'twant to use it in front of the other girls because of her condition. She said she wasn'tsure if she would need another sanitary napkin or if Cheryl had another one she could lether use. She said her mother had never discussed any of this stuff with her before.

"I'm sorry Myrisha, but I can't help you with that subject. Just ask Cheryl when shereturns to help you or give you some advice."

"Wendell, I can't do that," exclaimed Myrisha. "I'm supposed to be a woman. Ishouldn't have to ask somebody else about my own body. That's embarrassing."

I indicated to her that she was going to have to use it sooner or later.Myrisha opened the door, and exited the van. She started walking in the direction ofthe cliff's edge. The other four girls were returning in the direction of the van.

I turned the engine off and switched back to accessory power. The radio was stillplaying pop music. I heard Pat ask Myrisha where was she going.

Myrisha told her that she was going urinate. Myrisha then asked Cheryl to go with herso she would not be alone. Cheryl agreed.

The girls made it back to the van. Pat sat in the front seat this time. Diana sat in thesecond seat and Kimberly went to the back.

Just as they got seated, Cheryl could be seen approaching the van. She didn't get in butasked Kimberly to pass her tote to her. Kimberly reached the tote through the window,which was still open. Cheryl said in departing, "I have to go take care of my little daughter again."

After returning to her seat, Kimberly decided to stretch out on the back seat. Diana satwith her head leaning against the window that she had just closed. Pat had taken her shoesoff and had propped her feet up on the dashboard with the seat fully reclined. She hadher eyes closed and could not see me staring at those nice legs looking me in the face. Istarted thinking how different an experience it would have been if she had pulled up hershirt and removed her bra instead of Myrisha. Pat was already carrying a couple of grapefruits on her chest.

I started thinking to myself that I have to remember that these are little girls and thatthey are my students. Then I told junior to calm down. Junior was throbbing. To getmy mind off of the imposing figure seated next to me, I started thinking about what Iwas going to do with Josephine when I got home. I started pretending that the person nextto me was Josephine. My thought process was interrupted when Diana tapped me on theshoulder. I turned and asked her what did she need. At the same time Cheryl and Myrisha had returned to the van. Diana paused and waited until the other two girl got inthe van and got situated. Myrisha sat on the second seat next to Diana in the same spotwhere her womanhood had started. Cheryl told Kimberly to move her ass over. AfterCheryl got seated, Diana leaned over the back of my seat and asked me if I would help herwrite about out trip.

I wasn't sure what she wanted to write about. There were some things I thought would be better not mentioned. Some people might not understand.

"Diana, let's wait until we get back to school," I replied.

She simply said, "Okay!"

The next few minutes everything was quiet. Everyone was yawning and had theireyes closed. I was hoping that each of the girls would finally fall asleep.

CHAPTER SIX

As it got closer to daylight, the temperature began to rise a little. Not only was Ihungry, but I was tired and thirsty also. I remembered that I had a small bottle of waterunder my seat. I reached under the seat and found the bottle of water mixed in with acouple of other things that needed to be cleaned out from under there. I wiped the top offwith a handy wipe I had in my console and then opened the water. I took a sip or aswallow. It was only one of those six ounce sizes. With one swallow, two ounces wasgone.

Suddenly, Pat pulled her legs down from the dash and turned in the direction of the other girls behind her and said, "I guess we aren't good enough for some water."

Myrisha asked, "Do you have anymore water?"

"Sorry Myrisha, this is all I have."

Myrisha then asked, "May I have a sip please?"

Diana responded with, "It's too late. He's drunk from the bottle."

Myrisha snatched the bottle from my hand, turned it up to her mouth and sippedsome of the water. Cheryl asked Myrisha to pass the bottle to her. Myrisha passed thebottle to Cheryl who took a sip from the small bottle. She offered Kim the bottle and sherefused. Pat asked Cheryl to pass the bottle to her. Pat took the bottle and swallowed mostof what was left. She asked Diana if she wanted the last sip. Diana commented that shewanted some water, but could not drink out of the bottle that the others lips had touched.

Pat finished what was left in the bottle, thanked me and gave the bottle back to me.She then turned to Diana and asked, "What are you going to do when boys try to kiss you?"

Cheryl, who has the more humorous personality of the group

said, "She's going to puta napkin or a piece of paper between their lips.

A couple of the girls laughed.

Diana, not wanting to be laughed at alone, said, "Kimberly didn't drink any either."

Kimberly responded with, "I would have put my lips on the bottle if it had only beenWendell's and mines."

The other girls showed their disapproval by booing Kimberly's statement.

"There you go again," exclaimed Cheryl. "That man does not want you."

"I know what I feel," Kimberly responded.

"What in the hell do you feel?" Cheryl asked.

"She is probably feeling hunger pains," Pat added.

Before she could answer, the sound of what could be helicopter blades could be heardin the distance. It was now dawn and the van, being white in color, could easily be seenfrom the air.

I started the engine and turned on the headlights. Pat reached over and pushed myemergency flasher button.

No one said anything. Everyone just sat and listened. Finally, we could see theflashing lights from the big chopper as it flew overhead near the edge of the cliff.

I opened the door and walked to an opening where the pilot in the helicopter could seeme. I waved my hands back and forth. Finally, I saw a hand come out of the helicopterwindow and waved acknowledging that they had spotted us.

The helicopter hovered over the edge of the cliff for about a minute, and then flewaway.

There were lots of trees on this mountainside and I wasn't sure if there was enoughclearance for that big chopper to land. There were several clearances but they were all verynarrow.

I walked back to the van where all five girls were still seated. None of them got outof the van when the helicopter was flying above.

Myrisha asked, "Are we going to be rescued?"

I told her that we would be rescued shortly now that they knew where we were. I turnedthe lights and the engine off. The flashers remained on. As I had done earlier, Ireminded the girls how lucky we were not to have been in the path of those rocks andboulders. I suggested that we hold hands and say a thank you prayer.

Diana then asked, "Is it legal for us to pray like this. You know we are on a schooltrip."

Pat said, "Diana close your damn eyes and bow your head."

I reached out one hand to Diana and the other to Pat. Diana reluctantly grasped myhand and Kimberly's hand as we formed a crooked circle. Kimberly started praying and giving thanks for our past, present and future safety, reminding us that we weren't ho-meyet. Her prayer was short and sweet, not long and involved like a Cheryl's prayer.

Pat decided to leave the van to stretch her legs. Diana and Kimberly said they would joinher.

While the three girls headed away from the van, Myrisha com-mented to Cheryl that shewould not go on any more class trips, but only trips with her family. She also emphasizedthat she would be flying on her trips or traveling in the comfort of her mom's Navigator orher dad's limo.

"Well I'll be traveling with the band, basketball team and the track team next year,"remarked Cheryl.

Myrisha then asked Cheryl to go with the other girls and leave the two of us alone.

Cheryl laughed.

Suddenly, the sound of a helicopter could be heard in the distance again. I opened thedoor, got out and stood in front of the van. Cheryl and Myrisha soon followed.

Then the helicopter appeared. This helicopter was much smaller than the first one thatappeared. The copter circled over the trees and then landed in a clearance where thehighway intersected with the washed out roadbed.

Two men were in the helicopter. One was the pilot and the other was later identified asa military doctor. The doctor rushed over to where we were standing a few feet from the van. The other three girls had joined us. After I assured him that no one was hurt or sick,he informed us that the helicopter could only transport five people at a time. He said thatthey would take three of the girls first and then come back for the other two and me.

I asked him how long would we have to wait for the helicopter to return. He told us that they were only taking us to a waiting twelve passenger van about fivemiles on the other side of the rock slide. The van would then take us back to the school. I then instructed Patricia, Kimberly and Myrisha to take the first flight out. I thought Iwould feel more comfortable with Cheryl and Diana.

All three girls hesitated, probably wondering why I asked them to get on the first flight. The doctor appeared to have been in a rush. He assisted the girls with their gear andrushed them to the helicopter. In just a couple of minutes the girls and the copter wereout of sight.

I asked Cheryl and Diana to take all of their belongings out of the van and to check and make sure the other girls didn't leave anything.

I started searching my van to make sure I took everything out of it that I needed. Itook my gun case and some other items from my glove box and put them in a plastic bag.I locked the van and waited for the return of the helicopter with Cheryl and Diana.

There was no conversation between us as we waited.

Finally, after waiting for about ten minutes, the helicopter reappeared. It landed in thesame spot that it had landed in previously. We headed for the copter. Suddenly, Dianastarted pulling back. Cheryl boarded the copter. Diana stood near the door with her eyesclosed.

The doctor told me to get in. He directed me to the front seat opposite the pilot. Heput his arm around Diana and started talking to her. I couldn't hear what was being saidbecause of the noise from the helicopter. Finally, Diana moved toward the door and got in.The doctor sat next to her and they embraced each other tightly. Diana still had her eyesclosed.

I came to the conclusion that Diana was afraid to fly.

Shortly, we were airborne and headed home.

It was a short flight to where the helicopter took us. It was in the parking lot of a motel.But instead of taking us home in a twelve passenger van, a decision had been made to flyus home in the large helicopter that had first found us.

We all boarded the helicopter, fastened our seat belts and shoulder belts and headedhome. The flight took about forty minutes. Diana was still frightened. The doctor wasstill riding with her. He was constantly talking to her and her eyes were still closed.

Myrisha asked the pilots if they had anything to eat on board. They said they did not. Kimberly and Cheryl were very quiet and appeared to be nervous. They had never been inthe air before. Myrisha struck up a conversation with one of the pilots, making sure heknew that she had flown in helicopters and airplanes before.

Diana was not reading for a change. She was holding on to the book she purchasedfrom the tropical gardens. Patricia was sitting next to me with her head on my shoulder. She had her eyes closed as though she was trying to get some sleep. She smelled likeoutside.

It made me wonder how some men can sleep with a smelly woman.

As we approached the school, I could see a sizable crowd gathered along with a coupleof TV trucks.

The helicopter landed in the play area in back of the school. There were about twohundred people waiting for our arrival. We could not depart the helicopter until the blades stop rotating. As we departed the chopper, one of the school nurses, whoidentified herself as Hettie Mashburn, told us to walk through the line of people and gostraight to the cafeteria where the parents were waiting. Eight policemenescorted us through the crowd. Many of the people started applauding while otherswere calling our names. Many of the students who had returned the night before on thebuses, were also in the crowd. The TV cameras didn't seem to interest the girls as theyshowed little or no emotions.

When we arrived at the cafeteria, we could see all the parents waiting. Myrisha'smother ran and embraced her. Other parents followed suit. Personally I was looking forJosephine. I did not see her.

Mrs. Williams, our principal, came over to me and asked if I was okay. I told herthat I was but we needed some food and something to drink. She said it was Sundayand all of the cooks were off, but offered to buy us something to eat out of the school'spetty cash fund. She said she would take us to McDonalds or to Denny's, both locatednear by.

Just then Kimberly and her mother came over to me and her mother expressed herappreciation for taking good care of her daughter.

"Mr. Carter, Kimberly said you were real nice to her and took good care of her just likea father," Kimberly's mother said.

I thanked Kimberly.

Shortly after talking to Kimberly's mother, several of the other parents came over.Patricia's parents and Diana's mother came over together. They said they had beenpraying for us and that they were so happy to see their little girls alive and safe. Patricia'slittle brother said, "Mama don't forget you were crying too."

Myrisha's mother was there alone. She said her husband was in New York at aconvention and could not be there. Mrs. Moore invited me to come to her shop andpick out something for my mother, sister or girlfriend. I told her that it would not benecessary and thanked her anyway.

Mrs. Moore was very well dressed. I had to eye everything she was wearing. Myrishawalked to the Navigator with some man who must have been a chauffeur. Mrs. Moorecontinued thanking me and trying to get me to accept some type of reward or gift. Afterseveral refusals, she kissed me on the cheek and left.

I could certainly see Myrisha's personality in her mother.

I had morning breath and really became aware of it when Mrs. Moore kissed me. I madesure my mouth was closed. I went to the restroom in the cafeteria to rinse my month.

When I returned to the floor, I saw a reporter chewing gum. I asked him if he had anextra slice. He gave me one and I stuck it in my mouth.

My main reason for wanting the gum was, when Josephine arrived, I wanted a kiss in themouth, not on the cheek.Finally, Cheryl parents came over. Her dad was real cocky. He had been the one doing most of the talking to the reporters.

"What's happening brother? I'm Cheryl's father. I just want to thank you for takingcare of my little princess."

Cheryl and her mother both seemed a little embarrassed. Cheryl said, "Let's go get something to eat. I'll see you tomorrow Mr. Carter."

The girls and their parents left quickly, saying very little to the news media. Only Cheryland her father spent more than a minute conversing with the reporters. Mrs. Williams told me that the media wanted to talk to me. I was tired, hungry andsleepy. I asked her if they could come inside rather than me going outside. She said she would invite them in.

After speaking to the media outside the cafeteria door, Mrs. Williams invited thereporters in. After they entered the cafeteria, several of the reporters starting yelling outquestions at the same time. I intervened with my own yells telling them to be quiet.

"Just listen for a couple of minutes without interrupting me. I will tell you exactly whathappened during the last twenty-four hours."

I started with the three stops we made. I didn't give any details, just a quick generalization. Finally, I got to the part that they really wanted to hear, the part about theearthquake and the aftermath. I told them about the water and washed out road behindus, and the fallen rocks and the blocked road in front of us.

I told them about how nice and cooperative the girls were, and that they did not forgetto pray. I brought them all the way to the rescue. I closed with the landing of thehelicopter in the back of the school. Of course I left out the part about Junior and whatcaused

Junior to stretch several times, When I finished, I told them that I had to go getcleaned up and go find some breakfast.

Mrs. Williams, bless her soul, quickly asked the media to leave and started carryingsome of their equipment out of the cafeteria. In ten minutes, all of the media people hadgone or were leaving the campus.

Again Mrs. Williams asked me if I needed anything.

During all the excitement, I had forgotten that I didn't have a ride home.

"Mrs. Williams, I need a ride home."

"Sure Mr. Carter," she replied.

She locked the cafeteria doors and headed toward her car. She had an old GrandMarquis. When we reached the car, she asked me to drive because she did not knowwhere I lived, and she would get nervous driving and trying to follow directions at thesame time. I took the wheel, and was at my apartment in five minutes.

The first thing I did was to take off my strong smelling clothes. I threw them in thewashing machine with other clothes from the clothes hamper. I jumped in the showerand cleaned up real good.

I put on a pair of pajamas and headed to the kitchen. I had two hamburger patties in therefrigerator left over from Friday night. I warmed them up and scrambling a couple ofeggs. By the time I finished the eggs, the coffee and toast were ready.

The food tasted so much better this morning. Or maybe it's just seemed that way becauseI had been without it for a longer time than normally.

When I finished, I threw the dishes in the sink and went to bed.

CHAPTER SEVEN

ON MY RETURN home, one thing was really missing. I had not heard from Josephine. Ipicked up the phone and dialed her cell. She didn't answer. I had to leave her a voicemail.

Later during the day, I was awakened by the ringing of the telephone. I looked at theclock, and it was four in the afternoon. I had been asleep for six hours. I pickedup the receiver and said hello to the person on the other end of the line. It wasJosephine. She invited me over to her apartment for dinner. I accepted.

I got out of bed, went to the refrigerator and popped open a can of beer. I set mybedroom clock to alarm at 6:45 P. M. After finishing the beer, I got back in bed to getsome more rest.

It was 6:47 when I woke up. The alarm clock had been ringing for two minutes beforeit awaken me. I got out of bed, freshened up a little, put on some comfortable clothes andheaded for Josephine's apartment. I brought a bottle of coconut rum with me.

I rang the doorbell. Josephine must have looked out of the window or looked throughthe peephole, because she didn't ask who it was and opened the door immediately.

She closed the door behind me and locked it. The darkness in the apartment preventedme from seeing clearly what she was wearing. As we approached the dinning area, thelight made visible a beautiful multi-colored kimono that Josephine was wearing. Icomplimented her on how well she looked and how pretty her attire was. But I washoping at the same time that she wasn't planning on serving sushi to go along with thatkimono.

Josephine had a bottle of red wine chilling in the middle of the table surrounded by twoplace settings. I did not want to disappoint her by not liking what she had prepared, so Ithought I had better ask.

"What did you cook sweetheart?" Josephine responded, "Just wait and see!"

I intended to lay it on thick tonight so that the night might end in the bedroom.

I poured the two of us a glass of wine. While she was in the kitchen warming the food,I downed two glasses of wine. Finally, she brought the food in from the kitchen. She wastrying to make me feel at home. She had prepared catfish, white beans and rice and potato-salad. And of course she had my Pepsi.

Josephine put on some soft music and the stereo played while we ate. After we finishedeating, we danced a few times. Then Josephine pulled me by the hand and led me to herbedroom. She untied the sash to her kimono, opened it from the front and let it fall to the-floor. She had on a tight fitting see through pajama set. She walked over to the bed, inwhich the sheets had already been turned back, took off her slippers and eased in. Shereached back behind the bed and dimmed the lights with the dimmer switch. I walkedover to the bed, took off all of my clothes except my briefs, and got into the bed next toJosephine. After kissing a couple of times, she asked me to tell her about my trip.

Junior didn't want to talk about some trip. Junior was ready to take a trip.

Josephine is one of those analytical sisters. She reads all the time. I knew she was goingto worry me about every little detail. She re-minds me of Diana.

I started telling her in detail about the trip. She went from emo-tions of amazement toright out laughter. Josephine was fun to talk to. She seemed so interested in everything Iwas telling her. She had an out going, friendly personality like Cheryl's.

She stopped me in the middle of my story so that she could go and pour two more glassesof wine. While she was pouring the wine, I was observing how nice her bedroom was.Our apartments were in the same complex and were exactly the same size, but herfurnishings cost four times what mine cost. I was wondering how much she had paid forthe silk sheets I was laying on and for the comforter at the foot of the bed. Josephinedrives a BMW and can buy anything she wants. She didn't need any student loans or anything like that. But unlike Myrisha, she has never tried to use her money or herparent's wealth to influence me or anyone else. However, she does wear what I call thosefancy clothes and that expensive perfume like Myrisha.

When she arrived back at the bed, she handed me my glass of wine. Josephine sat onthe bed with her head leaning against the bed board and her legs propped up in the middleof the bed. Her pajamas were hanging low, exposing part of her buttocks. The light in thecorner showcased the contour of her breast in a silhouette against the wall. She asked meto continue where I left off with the details of my trip. It was very hard to concentrate.Junior was throbbing again like he was when Patricia had her legs propped up on mydashboard. As I journeyed through the trip, I continued to compare Josephine's legs toPatricia's. Both looked good but were shaped differently.

Finally, I got to the part where the helicopter picked us up. I was waiting for Josephineto get bored and tell me that was enough. But she listened intently as though she waslistening to Jack Ezra Keats, Delores Henderson or some other storyteller. She continuedto sip her wine from her crystal tumbler, while adjusting the position of her sleek body toenhance the curves at different angles.

Her hair, rolled in a bun earlier in the night, had slipped from its tie downs and washanging freely on her shoulders. I reached over a couple of times and let my fingers flowthrough the thick, black strands of hair. Josephine didn't complain about me playing inher hair. I guess Kimberly never had the right person to play in her hair. I bet she wouldhave enjoyed it if I had rubbed my hands through her hair while gazing into those prettyblue eyes.

Well, when I finished telling Josephine about the trip, we both sat our glasses down and got closer together under the comforter. She started kissing me on the neck and rubbingmy leg. Junior and I were waiting for her to involve him. Suddenly, she started pullingmy briefs off. I returned the action by taking off her pajamas, starting with the top. Aftersqueezing her breast for a moment, her bottom came off with one passage down her longathletic legs.

After several minutes of fondling each other, and after two years together, Josephinefinally said, "Put it in."

Josephine was the perfect woman for me. She was the best all around lady I had ever met. But during our sexual intercourse, images of Kimberly, Diana, Myrisha, Cheryl andPatricia kept entering into my mind. And at some stage, Josephine became each one ofthem.

I felt somewhat guilty or dirty as the images of the five girls kept entering my head. Iconsider myself a decent man, but I kept visualizing being with the girls for an extendedperiod of time. What if we had really been lost together, or if we didn't have to come backto East Orange County. Being in that environment with those students made me realizehow easy it would be to become a pedophile. I believe that the average man would havegiven in to some of the advances by the girls ignoring the fact that the environment hewas in was ideal for his control, but was only temporary. If not for laws, traditions and for the grace of God, our field trip could have easilybecome "PG-R" or "PG-X".

I guess I'll always wonder, what if?

I spent the entire night with Josephine. I went back to my apartment that morning,changed clothes and waited for Josephine to pick me up and drop me off at work.

The first day of school after the trip was no different from the previous Friday. All ofmy students were in class this day, including the five little girls that rode in my van. Ispoke to each of them as they arrived this morning. They all replied as they haddone all during the school session, "Good morning Mr. Carter."

I said to each of them, "Good morning."

THE END

Printed in the United States
By Bookmasters